EARLY PRAISE FOR
DARKNESS WITHIN

"*In* Darkness Within, *Hart spins fantasy creature lore in delightfully unexpected directions, then builds a suspenseful journey where main characters, Drew and Aideen, are as unsure about each other as they are about making it out alive. Add in plenty of will-they-won't-they steam and I'm impatient for more!*" - Poppy Minnix, Author

"*If you like Nalini Singh and Ilona Andrews, you'll love* Darkness Within, *a fantastic new novel from Cyprus Hart. Aideen and Druain are scorching hot together and take enemies-to-lovers to a whole new level.*" - Bestselling author Raisa Greywood

"*That was intense and funny all at once*". - J.L. Bowman, Author of *The Weekend*

DARKNESS WITHIN

Cyprus Hart

www.BOROUGHSPUBLISHINGGROUP.com

DARKNESS WITHIN
Copyright © 2021 Cyprus Hart

ISBN: 978-1-953810-57-1

4

To those who shone a beacon of light
when there was nothing but darkness

ACKNOWLEDGMENTS

There's no way I could ever thank everyone enough who's helped me along this journey. The last three years have been amazing, and I couldn't have done it without each and every one of you.

Poppy, for always being so encouraging, and for introducing me to the words and worlds of many different types of kissing books. One day I hope to be able to write characters with as much heart as yours.

Lori, for being nothing less than an über fan. Reading all those words I wrote at lightspeed and providing such helpful feedback. Keep writing all your wonderful stories.

A.T., for not only helping me improve my own writing, but for letting me grow my critique skills. Your descriptions are amazing.

Jackie, for many, many long discussions on complex and sometimes uncomfortable topics. The world needs your morally ambiguous vampires.

And to everyone else, all my friends in H&H, CP, WWLR, and TES, thank you so much for your friendship, kindness, helpful words, and fun times. You're all the best.

Also, thank you to my dog for making sure I walk at least a mile every day. I'm sure it's not at all motivated by your need to sniff everything, ever.

DARKNESS WITHIN

CHAPTER ONE

Aideen

My hands are shaking, there's a tense knot in my stomach, and I'm sure anyone with even the slightest sensitive nose can smell my anxiety from a mile away. This is the moment I've been working toward for over two years.

Costecu, the object of this raid, the stain on this city, is in the warehouse in front of me in a clandestine meeting with one of his top lieutenants. I have no idea what they're meeting about, and I don't care. The tip is solid, coming from the same inside informant who's been helping me and the organization I work for.

We're the only thing standing between humans and the evil represented by the two men inside that warehouse—Stephan Costecu, a hundreds-of-years-old vampire, and Druain Lindberg, his right-hand dwarf, a brutal enforcer and cleaner.

Along with the collection of misfits and malcontents they've gathered, they've been working every day and night to seed this city with chaos. The chaos they'll use to rise up against unsuspecting humans and take over.

In cities all across the globe, others are doing the same: a shadowy web of dangerous creatures who chafe under the weight of their lack of power. They long for the days when humans were prey: the servants, the chattel to be used and abused as wanted.

Those dark days are long past, old memories not even Costecu was alive to see. They were stopped by a group of creatures, who recognized humans would eventually have the numbers over "mythical" creatures like us. To survive at all, we needed to go into hiding. Maybe not the most altruistic of reasons to overthrow tyrants, but it worked out in the end.

The organization I work for is the distant descendant of that realization. If the world was the place I want it to be, I'd be able to have a regular job, take as many baths as I want, and never worry about being exposed as a selkie. All the turmoil that would arise from humans realizing their old fairytales and myths are true, at least to some degree, would be devastating.

Medusas would be weaponized, nymphs would be abused, dragons would be reduced to attractions you'd pay hundreds of dollars to see.

I shake my head, clearing the cobwebs away. No time to think about that sort of thing now. I need to focus on the task in front of me. Take one thing at a time and do my part to keep everyone safe.

"We're ready, chief," Jackson says next to me, peeking around the corner of the building at the side door to the warehouse. Our golem has finished setting the breaching explosives and is moving to a safe distance.

"I really wish you wouldn't call me that," I mutter over his head. At almost six feet, I've long gotten over being taller than even the average male, but Jackson is a gnome. He tops out at five feet tall, making the height difference more pronounced.

"Sorry, Miss Duffy. Habit."

"Aideen is also fine," I say, knowing he won't call me that. He's a soldier through and through, and while his professionalism means his squad is one of the best we have, it also makes me uncomfortable to be called "chief" or "miss." I'm not really in charge here. I investigate and coordinate, but I'm at home behind a desk, not out in the field. I couldn't miss this operation, though. I want to be here to see Costecu's face when we get him.

"Should I give the word?" Jackson asks.

"Sure. I mean, if they're ready. You know better than me. I'm here to watch."

"Okay. You sit tight. We'll have these bastards before you can sneeze," he says, winking at me and slipping around the corner.

The helmet and body armor I put on for safety are uncomfortable, one of the spare sets we have in case a desk jockey like me needs to go into the field. My dark braid trails out of the back of the helmet. I tug at the straps of the armor in another futile attempt to adjust it so it's not constricting parts not meant to be constricted.

Shifting from foot to foot to get out some of my nervous energy, I flick my gaze between the seven members of the squad, all different species and all trained to work with their special abilities. There's nothing else I can do now but wait.

They have all the information on who's inside. They know Costecu and Lindberg need to be taken alive, and they know anyone else in there is expendable. There will be deaths today, something I never enjoy planning for, but they're unavoidable. With any luck, they'll only be on the other side.

Jackson raises his hand, giving me a split second to duck back behind the corner before the explosion goes off. It's not like in the movies with a roaring thunder and flashing light and showers of rubble. That would attract far too much attention. Even though we're in a warehouse district that's long abandoned, it's still important to be as covert and quick as possible.

Our techs at the base will watch for any 911 calls, intercept them, and divert any response until we can get away clean, as long as we don't take too much time.

After the muffled thump, I wait a moment, and then look around again. There's a hole in the side of the brick building, and the phoenix and werewolf rush in—the point team. It's hard to kill the agile and strong werewolves, and even harder to put a phoenix down.

Gunshots pop from inside the building, no doubt those special incendiary rounds we keep for vampires, followed by some snarls and shouting as everyone else breaches the hole.

There's nothing I can do but stand out here and listen, crossing my fingers as I watch a tendril of smoke curl up into the blue sky. At least the building doesn't seem to be swarming with the opposition, which is my worst fear. Even though our mysterious mole has been accurate so far, I've always planned for the moment they aren't, perhaps getting discovered or forced to feed us bad information. This could've been a trap, but the noise inside dies down with each passing second.

For a moment, I imagine it could be because they've all been killed, but then Jackson pops his head out and waves me forward. I rush toward the jagged opening in the brick, stumbling over a chunk of debris, not used to wearing large combat boots.

While I'm still twenty feet away, I blurt out my questions. To my credit, I manage to ask about the team first, even though my brain is bursting with the answer to the second question. "Is everyone okay? Did we get them?"

Jackson sighs and rubs his chin. Recognizing the meaning behind the gesture, if not the exact answer, my stomach sinks.

"Well...partly," he says.

"Partly? What's that mean? You either get someone or you don't. It's not like you captured Costecu's feet." I'm on edge, but I shouldn't be taking it out on him. "Sorry. That was—sorry."

"It's fine, chief. Why don't you come with me? I'll show you."

I hate it when people do that. Just tell me what's going on. There's no need to "show" me anything, as if I won't believe it when told. I don't like to wait around.

Nothing good would come out of me saying all that, or protesting, so instead I bite my tongue and follow him across the concrete floor. A handful of charred vampire corpses are strewn about, and over to the side is a mangled joromungo.

Leftovers of whatever the building had housed lay along the edges, pallets stacked up and boxes tumbled on the floor like oversized cubes of salt. A layer of dust covers everything, disturbed into patterns of chaos where the fighting took place. Grimy sunlight filters through the windows below the twenty-foot metal ceiling. It's the exact place I'd expect a hidden meeting to take place, where the fates of many will be decided by evil men.

The phoenix is propped up against a metal I-beam near the middle, at the bottom of a set of rusty stairs. Our medic is tending to some sort of wound on her leg.

"You okay?" I pause to ask, not wanting to seem callous. Whatever unsatisfactory answer I'm about to get about Costecu and Lindberg can wait another ten seconds. There's no reason to make my reputation of being aloof any worse.

"I'm fine, ma'am," she says, somewhere between a grimace and a reassuring smile. "Pash'll get me patched up in no time."

"Glad to hear it." Something else seems warranted. "You did a good job today. Thanks."

"It's my job, but thank you ma'am."

Not sure if I sounded sincere, I turn and hurry after Jackson, who's waiting for me at the base of the stairs. They creak a little as we walk up them toward the enclosed room at the top. Must have been some sort of supervisors' office at one point, a place for all the managerial types to sit and watch over the workers who used to bustle about below.

He pushes the door open and gestures me in. The room is cluttered with papers and old office chairs, no walls except for the outside ones, desks tucked into corners, and for some reason all the phones unplugged and piled in the middle of the floor.

Those are the least important details, because struggling between our werewolf and golem, both of whom could win Olympic medals in weightlifting, is Druain Lindberg.

His face is mottled and red in anger, his coppery beard thrust forward and bristling, and he's spewing a litany of curses that stop the instant I walk into the room. His stare slams to mine like a magnet, and it takes all of my willpower not to step back. If looks could kill, I'd be a smoldering pile of ash on the floor right now.

"Who the fuck are you?" he snarls.

"She's the one who tracked you down, you piece of garbage," Jackson says, crossing his arms.

Before I can mount any sort of protest, Lindberg surges forward, ripping free from the grip of the two women holding him back. He's on me in an instant, huge and smelling like sweat and charcoal, towering above me and blocking out all of the feeble light. The back of my helmet hits the wall with a crash.

Pandemonium breaks out around me. Jackson is shouting, something crashes to the floor, hands are grabbing at Lindberg's shoulders, but my senses have tunneled down to the mountainous dwarf with his hand on my throat and the burning embers in his eyes.

"I'm going to fucking kill you," he growls, the sound cutting through everything else. "The first thing I'm going to do when I get out is find you and tear off all your tiny limbs."

I believe him. His muscles look like they have muscles, fighting for dominance under the button-down shirt he's got on. It's ridiculous I notice how well-styled it is, but they say when you're about to die your senses go into overload. I've given into my fate of being pasted against a dirty office wall when his grip releases.

The golem and werewolf jerk him away before anything else can happen, wrestling him down to his knees and then to the floor. The whole time he stares at me with a smug grin on his face, and I can't escape the feeling that he's letting himself get captured. With the ease at which he got away from them the first time, he could have snapped my neck in zero seconds flat.

I rub my hand across the skin where his thick fingers had grabbed and squeezed, sucking in air even though he hadn't choked me hard at all.

"Chief, are you okay? Chief."

I tear my stare from Lindberg as he's pinned to the floor, and glance to Jackson. "Yeah. Yeah, I'm fine."

"I'm so sorry. I'll make sure everyone gets a refresher course on restraining prisoners," he says, tossing a squinty glare over his shoulder. The werewolf scowls a little, the point of a fang poking out. The last thing I need is a pissed-off werewolf. They're hard enough to keep happy on a regular day.

"It's fine. They're doing a good job. It was an accident," I say, dropping my hand to my side while trying to regain some composure. I don't know if what I tell them will make a difference, but I ought to try. "They got him off me. Thanks, ladies. Let's get him in the transport."

"Don't try anything," the golem rumbles as she hauls Lindberg up, twisting his arm behind his back.

"Don't worry. You've got me fair and square." As they start to pull him out of the room, he leers at me with no shame,. The blatant nature of it makes me check to see if my clothes have fallen off or something. His shoulder passes mere inches from my face and I can't stop my head from jerking back.

"I'm guessing no Costecu." I turn and look at Jackson, resisting putting my hand out to lean against the wall. My heart is pounding fast after that scrape with death. I've been in worse situations a handful of times, but none felt as personal as Lindberg vowing to kill me. There's a difference between being shot at because you're in a fight, and being singled out for annihilation.

"Are you okay, chief?"

I appreciate the concern, but right now I need information. "Yes, I'm fine. Tell me what's going on."

"You got it. Yeah, no Costecu. Lindberg was waiting up here. Seemed real surprised to see us. Didn't say anything of substance until you showed up."

I nod. There's nothing else for me to do here. I walk down the stairs, Jackson behind me. The phoenix is standing, leaning against the pillar, looking worried. Jackson shoots her a look, and she closes her mouth on whatever she was about to say.

"Are you sure he didn't slip out a side door or something?" I shouldn't be questioning him, at least not in front of his squad, but I'm more disappointed than I've ever been. We were so close I could feel the end in sight, and now he's gone.

"Afraid not. Our spotter would have seen him. He's pretty good."

"Yeah. You're right. Yeah, sorry." My shoulders slump. Taking a deep breath, I push those thoughts aside and focus on the positive. We've got Lindberg, and he's no small fry. The information we can get out of him will be valuable. Costecu can only stay away from us for so long.

"It's okay, chief. We'll get him next time."

"Yeah."

The phoenix trails after us as we leave to head down the street a couple of blocks, and we load into the van. Lindberg is collapsed on the floor.

"He wouldn't calm down, so I dosed him," the medic says in response to my raised eyebrows. "It should last until we can throw him in a cell."

My mind is already planning the next steps. The ride back is quiet, which suits my thinking mood. As soon as Lindberg wakes up, I want to start questioning him, or at least build up a "relationship." Interrogation is a delicate art. You don't charge in with your metaphorical guns blazing, and Lindberg will no doubt be tougher than most. From what I know of his past, not much fazes him.

He's going to require a delicate touch and a lot of time. Those are two things that I do have. No matter how long it takes, I'm going to break into that brain of his and pull out every secret I want.

I'm not scared of him.

CHAPTER TWO

Druain

I wake in a concrete room that can only serve one purpose: containment. A large window stretches across one wall, although the only thing I can see is my face reflected back at me. After fifteen minutes of pounding on the thick one-way glass and shouting a string of curses and threats, I pace the cell. I need to be careful to stay in character, no matter my inner turmoil and confusion. A whole group of people could be on the other side, watching everything I do. Evil Drew needs to be on full display.

Running my fingers through my beard calms me inwardly, if not outwardly. I have a reputation as a fierce, angry, scary dwarf to maintain. To help hide my inner thoughts, I keep pacing and stomping, swinging my arms as if agitated and letting loose the occasional profanity.

I didn't expect a woman. I expected someone…rougher. Scars, white hair, maybe a broken nose. It was a bit of a shock to find out the agent who had been giving us so much trouble was a fairly attractive woman. Long black hair in a tight braid, and green eyes sparking like a live wire as she'd glared at me in the warehouse. The armored vest did a good job of hiding some curves, but I could tell they were there. She's tall, too, although still a good foot shorter than me.

She's been one small step behind us the whole time, causing so much trouble for Costecu. Killing or capturing most of his top lieutenants, appearing right on time to break up big deals and meetings, being a dogged and ruthless thorn in our side for years.

I want to give her the biggest hug in the world. She has no idea, but we've been partners since this whole operation started. I passed information to my handler whenever I could, and from there it went to Moarte. Every little leak I've been able to get out, she has followed with determination. I would know, since I've had to thwart her at every step.

Being buried in Costecu's army of misfits for over a year is getting to me. How much longer can I remain undercover and not break? I was about to come home, baiting Costecu into a fake meeting and leaking the details. It would have been the culmination of everything I've been trying to achieve, but then he didn't show, and now I have no idea what I'm going to do. I'm tired of pretending to be a monster and worried I may not be able to stop.

Costecu has a mole in with Moarte's people, although I'm not supposed to have that bit of info. No doubt the informant found out about the raid, which is why Costecu didn't appear. So then why did he let me get captured?

As I run through the possible reasons, worry rises to the surface: he's testing me. He wants to see how I'll act when I'm away from him. Does he suspect I'm not the perfect henchman I pretend to be? If he finds out my entire goal is to kill him and dismantle his organization, I'll be fucked. The mole will report back to Costecu on everything I do, I'm sure of it. I need to be as careful as a dwarf around dragons.

Or this could be some plan Costecu hasn't told me about, which is generally every plan. The man does not share much even with his closest advisors, like me. Maybe he let me get captured so I'd be able to do something. He'll have to expose his inside person to slip me orders, but Costecu isn't one to back away from risks. He wouldn't hesitate to get one of his henchmen killed delivering a message if it kept me in the dark until the last moment. If I don't know the plan, there's no way I'd be able to reveal it while under interrogation.

Interrogation. I'm sure I'll be interrogated. That's going to be rough. Staring across the table at the person we've code-named "Moarte." The one person who could probably help me, and I have to pretend I hate her, like I don't want to tell her everything so I can go back to living a normal life. A life where I'm not looking over my shoulder every second, where I'm not forced into doing things I still have nightmares about.

Except escaping to a normal life isn't possible. These years of blackness won't be for nothing. I'll go as deep as I need to see Costecu taken out. He's made me do terrible things, kill more people than I can count on my fingers or toes, and while I've mitigated the damage where possible, I've done stuff I'm not proud of. Giving up now, after all my work, would be worse than sticking with it to the end. I'll endure whatever other minor horrors are in store.

Pushing those thoughts from my mind, I focus on getting myself under control. I need to walk a careful line, and doubts and questions are dangerous. I need to be evil Drew without thinking, act as he would without hesitation. A pause or an unconvincing line could ruin everything.

I stomp harder, walk to the glass and bang on it again. I doubt anyone is watching anymore, but it'll help me get in character.

"Let me the fuck out of here," I shout. "Costecu is going to burn this place to the ground."

I doubt it, but it can't hurt to invoke his name.

"He won't let you keep me here. He's gonna swarm this popsicle stand like hell on earth. Let me out now and I'll make your deaths quick." I can see my reflection in the mirrored glass, and I'm satisfied with how my face turns red as I shout. I'd be scared of me. Instead of pounding the glass this time, I ram my fist into it. It's definitely reinforced, and the only damage I do is to my hand.

Growling like a caged manticore, I stride to the door and assault it instead. There's no doorknob, for obvious reasons, and the hinges are on the other side, but the metal makes a more pleasing sound when hit than the glass.

A few smashes later I've left a small dent and bloodied my knuckles. I ignore the red oozing from cracked skin. What kind of black-hearted, murderous dwarf would care about his bloody knuckles?

There's no furniture of any kind in the room. Three rapid paces take me along each wall. They're concrete, and I'd be willing to wager reinforced and thick. There are stronger creatures than me out there. I push against one wall, pitted and scarred from previous occupants, then lean a shoulder and shove, but of course nothing moves. The ceiling and floor are the same dull, grey concrete. A discolored patch in one corner catches my eye, where some blood, ichor, or venom was spilled, but it's old and it doesn't smell like anything.

Weak light comes from an LED bulb buried in the ceiling, with some heavy steel bars across it. I reach to grab one and give an experimental tug. It doesn't budge. I suppose I could break the bulb, but darkness and a cut hand would be the only things I'd get out of that. My night vision is good, but I still need at least a little light. I can't see infrared like some.

In one corner there's a dark hemisphere of plastic that must be the camera. I get right up under it, glaring into the opaque globe.

"I'm going to fucking crush you all with my bare hands," I shout. I doubt there's a microphone, but I imagine my expression conveys what I'm saying well enough. A few smacks with my fist leaves behind smears of fresh blood.

Back to pacing.

The adrenaline is wearing off, and whatever they shot me up with to knock me out is having some after-effects. My fingers feel thick, my head rests heavily on my neck, and I'm ravenous. Cold concrete's not the worst thing I've slept on, and I should probably try to sleep, but I can't. Sleep is the rational thing to do, and I'm not supposed to be very rational. I'm a big, dumb, punching machine, which is the only reason I got high up in Costecu's organization. He had me hit a lot of people, and I was good at it.

I keep pacing around in a square, pausing every few minutes to hit the door, or the window, or yell at the camera some more. It's boring, and I allow my body to run on autopilot, satisfied it'll operate without me needing to get involved.

Why would Costecu want me inside? He might want me to kill someone, or everyone. Capture someone. Information gathering isn't my strength, so I don't think he's going to expect me to memorize secret memos or anything. It must involve violence.

I'm so tired of violence.

Even if this is some kind of test, he's not going to come rescue me. He wouldn't want anyone near him who couldn't take care of themselves in situations like this. "Weakness is a disease, and I'm the cure," he says all the time. Instead, he'll have his mole spy on me, see what I do, and have a report ready by the time I get back.

I'm on my own until I find a way out of here. I'd like it to be without hurting anyone, but that may not be possible.

A sound so faint it's almost hidden under my heavy footsteps grabs my attention. I pause my marching. The light shifts with a sliver of movement under the door before a piece of paper comes shooting under it. I dash over and pound on the metal while trying to catch a scent, a clue as to whom it might have been.

"Hey," I shout, hoping for some reaction. "Get me the fuck out of here."

It's not what a smart person would do, drawing attention to the secret note they'd been passed, but evil Drew isn't smart. In fact, I'm hoping whoever reviews the security tape notices, and they can track down who was in the hallway.

The only response I get is silence, so I bend to pick up the paper, making sure to turn to face the camera, and hoping I'm not acting too stupid to be credible. It's folded in half and written on it in a craggy handwriting I don't recognize is two words:

Get Moarte

Well, that answers that. He expects me to kidnap and bring her back to him.

I shove the note in my pocket. Perhaps I can pass it off to whoever interviews me without getting caught, or them figuring out I passed it to them.

Well, shit. Handing Moarte to our nemesis isn't something I want to do.

I resume pacing.

What are my options here? If I get out and don't bring her back, he's going to kill me. If I don't get out, I'll spend the rest of my life in one of these cells. If I reveal I'm secretly working with them, and then they verify it with my handler, they'd pull me out, but then Costecu wouldn't have me thwarting him from the inside. I'll miss my chance for revenge.

If I get out and bring Moarte to Costecu, he'll kill her after a long and painful interrogation, setting me back a year with another death on my hands.

How many people have I brought to Costecu that ended up dead? I'd stopped counting. I've saved as many as I could, but it's not enough. As high-profile as Moarte is, the chances of me being able to get her away to safety are slim. Costecu will want to kill her personally, instead of getting me to do it like all the other times.

Sacrifice one more person into the grinder of personal revenge, or try to save her and doom countless others to terrible fates.

My stomach churns. These are the hard choices. This is why they accepted my proposal. No family, no friends, I'm fueled by nothing but a burning desire. A burning desire born from the ashes of my family and friends. Costecu killed them all, and he has no idea I got away. The only thing standing in my way of vengeance is one more person and a few more months.

It should be an easy decision.

I pace the room for hours until my feet hurt and my legs are sore.

The door opens revealing Moarte standing with her hands on her hips. Cheekbones I hadn't noticed before highlight the angles of her face. A waft of scent clean and sharp as the ocean teases my nose.

"Come with me," she commands.

My muscles tense to rush her out of pure instinct, but backup in the form of the humongous woman of a golem and the lanky werewolf who took me down in the warehouse bracket Moarte's shoulders. I could take one of them, but not both at once, and if I'm unconscious I can't do anything.

"Why?" I demand, lowering my head to glare at her, testing the waters of her patience.

"Grab him," she says with a hint of satisfaction, stepping aside to let the two enforcers in.

I sigh to myself and put up a good fight. By the time they finally subdue me I've broken a couple of the werewolf's fingers, but in exchange I'm pretty sure all the ribs on my left side are snapped. I've even managed to hit the golem in the face, but I don't think it did anything besides crack my knuckles open again.

They drag me out of the room, along a few blurry hallways, and then into another room. Similar to the last one, but bigger, with a metal chair bolted to the floor.

Heavy leather bands are strapped across my arms, legs, and chest, securing me in place. I could get out, but not before they stopped me.

The werewolf bashes me in the side of the head before they leave, showing her teeth in what is far from a smile, and I'm left facing Moarte alone.

She leans back against the glass and crosses her arms over her dark blazer.

"Let's talk," she says.

CHAPTER THREE

Aideen

Lindberg stares at me like I've told him I punched his mother, and he doesn't say a thing. I didn't expect him to. It's not like I thought I'd walk in and he'd spill all his secrets.

I didn't sleep much last night. Too much adrenaline from the raid, and too much disappointment from not grabbing up Costecu. I soaked in my tub until the wrinkles on my fingers had wrinkles, but it was cold comfort. After climbing into bed with a glass of wine, I went over my notes on Lindberg before falling into a fitful sleep, haunted by dreams of him advancing on me with his huge hands flexing.

I woke up in a cold sweat, took another bath, and got dressed. The sun was rising as I drove into the office.

Now I pace back and forth in front of him, pushing those dreams from my mind and trying to decide how to proceed. Maybe time and silence will get under his skin. Everyone has their own pressure points, and sometimes it takes a while to figure them out. I'm patient. It's not always the most pleasant aspect of my job, but it can be rewarding. The high when someone you've been working on gives you a critical piece of information—there's nothing quite like it. I'll wear him down, and when I do he'll spill all his secrets. I've waited years for a big break, and while this could've been bigger, I'll work with what I've got.

I stare at my feet, pacing and pretending to think. As if I haven't thought about this scenario a thousand times. Tilting my head to the ceiling, I let out a big breath, still walking in measured paces. His gaze is a hot hammer pounding at my nerves and setting them on fire. Stopping in front of him, I turn and make eye contact. His eyes burn fire, but I won't be intimidated, leveling my own hard glare right back. I wait to see if he'll say anything. He doesn't.

They say whoever speaks first loses the advantage, but that's not always true. As long as you keep the power for yourself, it doesn't matter what the words are. He has power because we need him, need his information. I have power because I can make his life easier or harder at my whim.

"Why do you think Costecu abandoned you?" I'll start with the assumption Costecu wanted to get rid of him. Sow seeds of dissent. Even if only one grows, it's a seed that wasn't there before.

He doesn't answer, his gaze fixed on mine.

I didn't expect anything, and there's no point in pushing this now. His adrenaline is pumping from the fight, he's angry, and though he doesn't notice it yet, he's going to ache where Alice and Abi banged him up. I'll let him sit for a while to calm down and see how he reacts to whatever pain comes.

"To be honest, I'd be disappointed if you started talking right away. That's not fun, is it?" I ask, turning away and walking out without looking back. The door clangs behind me, and I stand still for a moment before relaxing. I walk around the corner to peer through the one-way window.

Jackson, the safety man in case things went bad this round, sits next to me at the table. Any sort of escape attempt and he'd lock the door with the press of a button until backup arrived. "Think he's gonna be hardheaded, miss."

"No doubt, Jackson. No doubt."

Lindberg is staring at the glass, right where I'm standing. He's no fool. It's a pretty safe assumption I'd be looking at him, and he's not going to reveal any emotion but fury. I move to the side a little to get out of his direct line of sight. A tiny move to assure myself he can't really see me. His stare is molten.

"He's not going to do anything," I say, turning away. "I'm going to go review some notes. I'll be back in an hour. You want to watch him until then, just in case?"

"Sure thing," Jackson says, kicking his legs onto the table, settling back to wait.

"Thanks. See you soon."

I stride off down the hallway, heading to the elevator. As I wait for it to arrive, I lean on the wall and slow my breathing. Being around Lindberg in person sets off all my alarms. By far, he's the most dangerous of all Costecu's minions we've captured, and to have him dropped into our lap like this is a huge stroke of luck. It seems too good to be true.

The elevator opens to reveal Frank, my assistant. "Hey, Aideen. Coming to get you, see if you needed anything." He holds the doors open for me, then pushes the button for floor fifteen, where our offices are.

"How'd you know where I was?"

"I figured you'd be down here, studying your newest puzzle."

"Yeah. Actually, I could use a bagel and a coffee. I'll be in the coffee shop if anyone needs me. Have you updated the spreadsheet and put Lindberg on there?" I tap the button for the lobby, needing some time around humans. Regular people who can't kill me without breaking a sweat.

"Yup. All done and ready for review."

"Thanks." The elevator dings a tone market research decided was pleasing for most species. To me it sounds like an off-tune bell.

The doors open onto the lobby, a shiny expanse of marble and glass. None of the people who live or work here suspect we're under their building. No one looks twice at another office drone dressed in a tie or work blouse, even if they happen to be seven feet tall or have bright green hair.

Making my way over to the small cafe, I order a chocolate chip bagel and splurge on a latte, the breakfast of champions. Sitting at a table where I can observe the ebb and flow of people, I reflect on their fragile lives. At any moment, a crazed creature could come tearing through and end any of them, and no one has a clue.

The bagel disappears too quick for me to savor, and I have no excuse not to get up and take the remains of my latte to my office. Riding in the elevator, I meet the morning staff coming in and the night staff leaving. Weaving through the halls on the way to my little corner of the floor, I greet and nod at people I know. Frank is typing away at his computer, pretending to work, but I bet he's flirting with the leprechaun in R&D. As long as he does his job, I have no desire to micromanage.

Settling into my leather chair, I open my laptop, review the sheet of who we've got contained, then pretend to do other work while pondering this turn of events.

Costecu not showing up was unlucky, but something about it feels off. Why would they meet at some random warehouse, and who would know about it to leak it to us? They've got a base of operations, although we haven't located it yet, so why meet in a less secure location?

The more I think about it, the more unsettled I become. Something doesn't feel right, and I can't afford to be unsure.

My latte's gone cold. I toss it into the trash and swivel back and forth in my chair, trying to resist the temptation to head back to the basement and grill Lindberg more. Giving up after five minutes of struggle, I close my laptop and pull it from the dock, carrying it with me. The detainment floor is empty of staff. There aren't many prisoners in-house at the moment. My footsteps produce a muffled echo in the quiet halls.

Jackson looks up as I enter the room. "Back so soon?"

I stare at Lindberg through the glass. The dwarf is huge, must be nearly seven feet. When he's sitting, he's almost eye to eye with me, and I'm not a short woman. He must weigh a figurative ton. What I can see of his neck behind the beard is thick, holding up his square head.

His eyes, a muddy shade of brown, still stare at the same spot on the window, like he's trying to melt a hole in the glass with pure rage.

"Something's not right with this," I reply, shifting around to stay out of his line of sight. "It's practically a gift, him falling right into our laps."

Some sort of tattoo peeks out from under the sleeve covering his massive left bicep. I wonder if he's got any more, and if they mean anything special to him. I was close to getting a tattoo once after a night of drunken karaoke with my old college friends. They tried to get me to have the kanji for "dedication" tattooed on my inner wrist, but at the last minute I backed out.

His beard isn't wild and bushy, which would match his personality, but instead it's average size, perfect to sink fingers into, and definitely under tight control. Combined with his cutting-edge haircut and trendy clothing, he wouldn't look out of place in the regular population. In fact, he's fairly good looking, and doesn't appear to be crazy or murderous. Except for those intense eyes.

I blink and shake my head, trying to break whatever weird spell is threatening to fall over me.

"Not sure, chief," Jackson says, breaking my thoughts, and I try to remember what I asked him. "Not really my specialty, all that planning and plotting. I'll stay with the physical side of the business."

"You're good at it." An idea strikes me. "Any insights while you've been here? He's an enforcer too. I mean, not that you're like him," I amend, not wanting to sound condescending.

Jackson chuckles, relieving me of my embarrassment. "It's okay, chief. I know what ya meant." He stands, moves around to my left side. "He's been staring at that spot in the glass. Hasn't moved a muscle. If it were my guess, I'd say he's either really dumb, or really clever at being dumb. Since he's been working for a while before getting caught, I'd wager on the last one. No one's dumb enough to be that blank. Be careful. You want me to send someone down to watch? I gotta get my reports written."

Letting Jackson's words sink in, I keep my eyes on the dwarf in the chair, bound and unmoving. He's right. No one could cause us so much trouble for this long without a whole host of skills. It's easy to try to reduce people to simple terms, especially if they're doing horrible things, but they're still people. People who want to shape the world into fitting their desires and wants. People who are fighting for what they think is right. What does he think is right in that skull of his?

"Oh, yeah," I reply, coming out of my thoughts. "Don't worry about sending anyone. Nothing's going to happen. I'll probably let him sit for a while. See what a day of being hungry and achy does."

"Sure thing. Good luck."

"Yeah," I mumble to the closed door, rolling the chair back a little before I sit. In the silence of this dim little observation room, I lean forward and study his face. Perfectly blank, not a feature shifting out of place. If he's hurting, he's not showing it.

Did Costecu throw him to the wolves? Maybe he did something to piss off his boss, but then why let us snatch him up instead of killing him? It might be a trap. Maybe he wanted to get captured, or was ordered to get captured. I wouldn't put it past them to try something sneaky.

He's still staring at the glass without a hint of life or movement. The need to get in his head and see what's going on in there, to understand what's motivating him, is intense. I hope there's some sort of trauma in his past, something horrible to make him this way, because I'm not sure what I'd do if he enjoys causing pain for fun. Those types of people are unfathomable.

Getting up to pace the room, the need to understand this dwarf keeps growing. I should be patient, take my time, follow protocol, but the burning inside demands answers. What makes Druain Lindberg tick?

The room isn't big, and it only takes a few steps to go between the two walls, one lined with a metal shelf. Back and forth. I shouldn't go in there with him. I'll learn all his secrets soon enough. His eyes don't move, and there's no way he can see me, but the heat of his gaze is challenging. Back and forth. What could he really do? He's secured. No one's escaped yet. Patience is a virtue and all that.

It would be smart to judge his condition, though. Make sure he's not seriously hurt, check the ribs Alice snapped. He's not good to me if he dies of internal bleeding.

It would also be a good idea to hear him speak, whether I get anything out of him or not. The best way to start building a plan against him is to see how he acts and reacts. Facts on a screen are one thing, but talking to someone, being face to face with them in the same room can teach me so much more.

I give in to my curiosity.

Not bothering to call someone to watch, because I'll only be in there for a few minutes, I step to the door and swing it open. His eyes don't waver, still staring at the same spot in the glass as before, and I glance over to make sure he can't really see through it. All I see is my reflection.

A couple of steps take me in front of him, and then he moves, his gaze rising to meet mine. It's no softer than it was before, boring into me with the sharpness of diamonds.

"So why are you the way you are? Who hurt you to make you into a killer?" I ask. It's a useless question, but maybe it will provoke something from him.

Still nothing, not a flinch in those eyes. No hint he's either proud or ashamed of what he's done.

"I don't really care. I'm curious about you, that's all." Don't feed whatever ego he might have. "Not even you, specifically. I'm curious about people in general. We grow up in different ways, live different lives, and meet different people. Some rise from the bottom, and some sink from the top. Why? Why do you think you're the way you are?"

The tug of his gaze is strong, but I keep my eyes forward. "Do you even know how many people you've killed?"

"Not enough," he says, catching me off guard. His voice is low, much more contained than when he was shouting with rage. It sounds like granite, and promises violence, like an avalanche.

"Not enough? You want to kill more people?" I ask, stopping in front of him, schooling my face into a neutral expression. I'll let him say what he wants and won't allow him the satisfaction of being provoked.

"At least one more." His lips move as if pronouncing my doom. A horrible metallic screech rends the air and a flash of realization surges through my brain. I barely have time to curse myself for being so careless before he barrels headlong into me, the chair torn from the bolts in the floor.

All the air is dashed out of my lungs as I'm smashed into the glass. A massive splash of pain rings through my head as it snaps into the mirror, and everything goes dark.

CHAPTER FOUR

Druain

A lump of regret hits my guts as I rip the chair out of the floor and smash Moarte into the wall. I really need to use her real name. Whoever was watching didn't notice me rocking back and forth as slow as I could to test and then loosen the bolts fastening the chair to the floor. The bolts must have been in there a while, because they came up without a lot of effort.

I don't really care if anyone is watching. Maybe they are, and they'll come storming in here in ten seconds. I'm gambling I can take on anyone who shows up while I'm still strapped to this chair. If I am overpowered, at least I made a statement. Stayed in character.

I bash the back of the metal chair against the wall a few times, sending reverberations through my spine. After a few whacks something loosens and I manage to twist the chair apart, freeing myself from the restraints. No one's come to rescue her yet, which seems strange. They must have protocol to protect against things like this. Perhaps she broke it.

It looks like I have a legitimate escape on my hands. All the better. I need to get out of here before I do or say something wrong and ruin my cover. Getting back to Costecu and figuring out his plans is my top priority. This situation is too far out of my control. I run my fingers through my beard to try and stay calm as I think.

Kneeling, I give her a few gentle slaps to the face. I need her conscious for this. I shove aside the building guilt, cramming it into the box where I put anything not angry and scary. Focus on the goal. Get into Evil Drew's headspace.

One more tap and she cracks her eyes open. Sharp and green, they focus on me instantly. I slap her for real, and those emeralds slam open further. If I'm reading her right, she's more angry than scared, which makes sense. She must have nerves of steel to be in this business.

"Get the fuck up. You're helping me get out of here," I say, grabbing her upper arm and hauling her upright. The top of her head rises to brush under my chin. I could toss her over my shoulder and carry her out with ease, but I'm hoping to be able to use her as a shield. A butt and a pair of legs dangling in front of me won't protect much.

"You won't get away with this," she hisses at me, tugging back, trying my strength. I don't budge an inch and laugh in her face.

"I think I already have. Forgot to call for backup? You fucked up."

She glares back, her gaze piercing me further than I'd have thought possible. She's intense, not nearly as scared of me as I'd hoped, and I have to fight my worry. This would be so much easier if she'd snivel and plead for me to let her go, turn to putty and let me control her. Goddamn it.

"They'll stop you before you make it ten steps," she says as I drag her toward the door. It opens at my push, not locked from the outside. She really screwed up. Coming in here must have been an impulse, something she wasn't planning on doing. From what I remember from her file, she's not the reckless type, and this seems out of character. Maybe they're feeling the pressure from Costecu, desperate to get results, or maybe she couldn't resist my handsome face.

"Which way is out?" I demand, changing my grip to her wrist, fingers circling it with no problem. A stray thought surfaces, wondering what type of soap she uses to get such smooth skin.

"Fuck you."

I turn and smack her across the face again, not too hard, but enough to make it sting. Her hand flies up to her cheek and her eyes narrow in anger. My stomach turns every time I have to hit a defenseless woman. I'm down for a fair fight, like against the hulking golem, but slapping Moarte is something I don't enjoy. There's not a thing she could do to hurt me.

"If you think I won't hit you because you're a woman, think again," I growl in my most menacing tone, ignoring the hard knot in my chest. "Don't fuck with me. Which way is out?"

She says nothing, glaring back with those bright eyes, until I raise my hand again.

"Left." Her chin juts out in defiance.

It's a dangerous spark I should snuff out before it gets me or her killed, but I can't quite correct it. "If you're lying, I'm not going to go easy on you."

"Oh, please," she scoffs, stumbling behind me as I drag her along. "It's not going to go good for me no matter what. You're taking me right to Costecu, like the good lapdog you are. Maybe he'll give you a treat. Puppy want a treat?"

I grit my teeth and ignore her obvious attempt to get under my skin, passing by more two-way windows revealing empty rooms. Coming to another T in the hall, I turn, eyebrows raised, and wait. The only response I get is another hard glare, a pair of green lasers trying to cut me in half, so I slap her again.

"Don't make me ask."

"Right," she says, jaw muscles flexing. Her hand twitches, no doubt resisting the urge to rub the blooming red.

"Good girl." I yank her after me.

"What? I'm not...I'm not a girl, you patronizing ass."

"Whatever you say, sweetie." I'm careful not to turn and let her see the grin tugging at my mouth. I've found a button to push.

"I'm not your fucking sweetie, either. Left," she says, this time only requiring a look from me.

"You learn fast, darling. What should I call you then?"

"How about fucking nothing. As soon as they figure out you've taken me, everyone's going to descend on you and take you out."

"Let them come, Fucking Nothing. Too long. I like Zero." I squeeze her wrist tighter and turn to give her a lewd wink.

"Of course you would. You're a real piece of work. To the right. You're hurting me," she protests, tugging at my hold in an adorable attempt to get away.

Not bothering to respond to the complaint, I pull up when an elevator comes into view. "What's this? You want to trap me? No. Stairs."

"There aren't any." She looks at me in supreme smugness. This woman's got stones, I'll give her that. She hasn't shown an ounce of fear, though she has to know my reputation. Admirable.

"Bullshit."

"You think we haven't thought of this? Or you're so special you're the first one to attempt an escape? We can cut power and leave you stranded, no way out but trying to climb up the elevator shaft. No one's made it out yet."

"Yeah, except you broke the rules, and no one knows I've escaped," I throw back at her, mashing the button with my thumb. "So we get to use the elevator. When it opens and I've got my hand around your neck, they're going to let us go."

"Please," she laughs at me. "They'll kill me to kill you."

This stupid elevator is taking forever. I smash the button a few more times. "Works for me. I'd be glad to trade you for me. I'm nothing." It was a lie, we both knew it was a lie, but it was partially the truth. Costecu would recover a lot quicker than Zero's people would. He'd gladly let me die to get rid of Moarte, which worries me *a lot*. Maybe that was the whole plan from the start.

The doors open and she puts up a little fight, trying to pull back, but I drag her into the elevator. It's far too bright and shiny, every surface a metallic mirror. No matter where I look I can see my face, a fierce scowl stretched across my features. Zero's eyes widen in a brief moment of concern, but the mask of anger slides back into place moments later. In the brief sliver of transition, her face smooths out and I'm caught by how attractive she is. Classic beauty in every sense of the word. It's a shame what's going to happen to her. It takes a great effort to keep my face from twitching over to something less than scary.

Her eyes flick, and I grab her free wrist as it darts out to punch the emergency button on the pad. A quick twist of her arm behind her back and a push against the back of her neck, and I've got her smashed against the metal wall of the elevator.

"Don't get yourself killed," I growl into her ear, being sure my hot breath hits her skin, trying my hardest to drive any bit of fear into her. She has the guts to struggle against me, her free hand planted on the wall to push back, and only then do I notice the position we're in.

Her whole body is wriggling against me in a futile attempt to get free, head turned to glare. Her butt is pressing against my crotch, and even through the several layers of material, it's obvious how tight it is. I can't control my body's reaction, but control is not something

Evil Drew is familiar with. It would be so inappropriate to do anything else, so that's exactly what I do.

Taking my hand off her neck, I grab her chin and pull her head back, smashing a kiss onto her mouth. I enjoy the outraged sound she makes against me way more than I should, and come away tasting cherry lip balm. "You're cute. Keep struggling, Zero."

If I thought she looked angry before, it pales to the fury crashing over her face now. "You disgusting piece of shit. Do that again and I'll bite you until you bleed."

"So why didn't you?"

Her glare is becoming familiar, little wrinkles between her eyebrows. I smirk and reach for the button with the star, figuring it to be the ground floor. "Here's what's going to happen. The door is going to open, and I'm going to walk right out the front, and if you try to signal something or talk to anyone, I'll start breaking your fingers."

"Screw you."

Flipping aside her hair, I run my nose up the back of her neck, inhaling her clean scent. "I barely even know you, Zero. Let's at least get coffee, first." Enjoying her little noise of indignation, I grab her around her neck from behind, still with her arm twisted between us, and peel her off the wall to face the doors. "Wish us luck."

With a pleasant ding, the elevator slides open and I stride out, no hesitation. The lobby is marble and glass, fancy and expensive looking. I shove her in front of me before striding forward. At first no one notices us, but then one person does, then another, and quickly everyone is staring.

"Let us through, and I won't kill anyone," I shout out. No need to be subtle anymore. "Try to get in my way, and I *will* kill everyone."

"Don't list—"

I cut her off with a hard squeeze to her neck. Her attempted instructions end in a gurgle. "What did I say, Zero? Did you already forget?" I put light pressure on her wrist as a reminder, not wanting to do serious damage, but needing to get back into the bad-guy groove.

People part in front of us as I keep walking, head on a swivel to check for any threats. I'm surprised at how lax security is here, until I recognize the building we're in.

"Really? You're hiding underneath the Connor Tower? Mixed-use offices and condos? That's pretty smart, actually," I concede. "Wouldn't notice the extra power, established building. I bet you're regretting the lack of security out the front door right now though, huh?"

Her throat vibrates as she grunts something, and I release the pressure on her a little.

"Go to hell," she replies.

I chuckle, and feeling cheeky, bite the shell of her ear to hear her grumble again. "You're already there, Zero."

A lone, young security guard materializes in front of us, the last obstacle to the outside, his hand resting on what appears to be a taser. I raise my eyebrows.

"Really, kid?" I ask with no menace. I shouldn't need it for this. "You're going to try to stop me? I could break you in half with one hand." Zero tugs against me, perhaps thinking I'm distracted enough to weaken my grip.

"Don't even bother, Zero," I growl into her ear. Her scent is starting to wilt along with her demeanor, the stiffness of resistance leaking out of her limbs. "I could drag you around by the neck with one hand while I snap the spine of this wet noodle, and still have time to get a bagel. What's your favorite flavor? I'll get you one, too."

I keep stalking toward the guard. To his credit, he doesn't move aside until the last minute. I would have walked right over him.

"Good choice. Stay alive to tell your girlfriend or wife how you were so heroic today, standing up to a big, strong, nasty man. Get yourself laid. Open the door, Zero."

She doesn't move, instead tensing up against me. Perhaps the adrenaline is wearing off and she's realizing how much trouble she's in. I twist her wrist a half-inch further.

"Open the door, Zero. My hands are full. Sorry, but I don't quite trust you enough to let go." I suppose I could push it open with my foot, but part of me enjoys the thought of making her continue to aid in her own abduction. "Open the door. Your delicate fingers would break really easily."

A second of hesitation more, and I'm steeling myself to follow through with my threat, but then she pushes the door. Stifling my sigh of relief there's no need to break any delicate part of her yet, I keep her facing the guard as we back out of the building. I'm not so stupid as to think he won't taze me in the back.

It's not quite noon, a nice and warm summer day, and as the door shuts I let go of her arm and keep her close with my arm around her waist.

No need to look suspicious outside and draw more attention.

No doubt the cops are already on their way.

I need to steal a car.

CHAPTER FIVE

Aideen

His arm around my waist is huge and pulls me against him in the way a man would hold his lover instead of his captive and enemy. The hairs on his arm might as well be sandpaper as they brush against a tiny triangle of skin above my hip. I get the feeling he could smash me against him, but instead I'm only caged between his arm and chest. The closeness of his body heat is unbalancing, an intimate sensation I don't want to feel from this monster. My cheek still stings from the slaps, but I refuse to give him the satisfaction of rubbing it.

Even knowing the details in his file, being up close and personal makes it all the worse. His horrible musky smell, no doubt from all the adrenaline and not washing the last couple of days, wafts over me, inescapable and almost tangible.

I try to push away from him, a hand on his chest, but he doesn't move or loosen his arm one bit.

"Try all you want. You aren't getting away," he says, smiling under his beard and pulling me down the stone steps toward the street.

Where's he going? I hope someone inside called the cops at some point. "If you don't let me go, I'm going to scream."

"Go right ahead. You think anyone's going to stop me? That I'm going to end up on some sort of naughty list?" He laughs loud.

Of course. He's already on every list he could be on. He's not a criminal, he's an actual terrorist. My quest to bring him and Costecu to justice isn't exclusive. Even the regular authorities have Lindberg on their list. Still...if I got some attention maybe someone would slow him enough to give the cops time to arrive.

As if reading my thoughts, he shuts down hope. "I'll kill anyone who tries to stop me," he says in my ear with a jovial undertone. "I don't have time to fuck about with more delays. You really want the blood of some innocent civilian on your hands?"

I'm dragged across the sidewalk, drawing stares. Looking at the passing faces, I can't bring myself to put someone in danger. It was because of my fuck-up he got out. I won't destroy any more lives to make my future easier. But I don't need to make his life easier either. I turn my head and chomp into his arm, clamping my jaw as hard as I can, feeling strong muscle squish between my teeth.

He grunts, then laughs. "Aren't you playful." Without breaking stride, he jams his thumb between my teeth and pries my jaw open. His fingers grip under my chin while his thumb presses on my tongue. The salty taste of his skin invades my senses, and I splutter and hack, trying to swallow or cough.

"Don't do that again, Zero." He lets go.

I gulp and then spit on the ground. "So where are we going?"

"Right here's good." He stops in front of an old pickup. "Cover your eyes."

Without even looking around, he jams his elbow into the passenger-side glass. A crack, another crack, and then a final one before the window gives way in a sparkling explosion. I cover my eyes after the fact, shocked he's so brazen. A couple of people nearby shout, but he doesn't look up or even flinch. Blood drips out of a sizable gash in his elbow.

Reaching inside, he pops the lock, opens the door, and then pushes me inside. "Open the other door for me. There's a good girl."

I glare at him, but he leans forward, shoving his face inches from mine. His breath is hot, and smells like something I can't quite place. It reminds me of darkness and menace. Blinking, I force myself not to back away.

"Open the door or I'll kill people, starting with the clown looking like he's going to try something." He turns his head to stare out the front window at a large, but not large enough, man staring at us.

Lindberg pulls his head out, smiling at the man with teeth only, and walks around the front to the driver side. "Lost my keys," he explains. It's not convincing.

For a split-second I hesitate, wanting to call out for help, but then he's at the driver-side window, tugging on the handle.

"Open the door up for me, babe." His mouth is still smiling, but his eyes are the same intense gaze he leveled at the glass back in the interrogation room, what seemed like hours ago.

I reach across and open his door.

The truck rocks down as he slides onto the seat with surprising agility, his head an inch from brushing the roof. "Good girl." He grins when I open my mouth to protest. "Sorry. Good Zero."

He pats my knee, and I jerk it away, disgusted. The heat lingers from his hand, and I wish I had a cloth, or maybe some steel wool, to scrub away the tingling feeling.

He fiddles under the dash, and the truck coughs to a start. If I get out of this, I'm adding grand theft auto to his list of crimes just because I can.

As he pulls out of the parking spot, hope begins to spiral away. I need to get my thoughts and emotions in order for whatever lies ahead. I'm sure it'll be bad. There's no doubt they're going to interrogate me. My only question is for how long and how hard. Will they go right to teeth pulling, or begin smaller? I try to remember the protocol for situations like this. Make up lots of stuff so they can't tell what's true, and while they're busy being confused, wait for rescue. If rescue doesn't seem possible, try to piss off the interrogator so they'll kill you and end the torture.

I have a tracker injected under my skin at the hip. Every agent does. It can be useful for situations like this, or finding and identifying a body. Seeing where I'm being taken would be good intel, but I'd rather not wait to find out what's in store for me. I have minimal training in things like this. I'm a desk jockey, not a field agent.

As we roll to a stop at a red light, I grab the door handle and push, a lightning bolt trying to find ground. The door flings open, but a steel grip clamps my upper thigh and yanks me back into the seat before I can escape.

"Close the door, Zero. Don't want to look all damaged in front of Costecu. He'll think I've mistreated you, and we can't have that, can we?" His fingers dig into my skin, wrapping all the way around to the inside. If he moved his pinky up half an inch, I'd be able to charge him with sexual assault on top of grand theft auto. The fabric of my slacks does nothing to dampen the heat of his hand soaking into my skin, and I want nothing more than to pull away. I don't, and instead I glare at him for a moment before slamming the door shut.

"Good choice, Zero. Good choice." The locks click, and I consider jumping out the open window, but his hand doesn't move from my thigh even as we drive off. It feels like a vise has me clamped in place.

He keeps pace with the afternoon traffic, not doing anything to draw attention. As we pull up to the next stoplight, he shuffles his hand around in the pocket on the driver side door, then turns to me. "Open the glove box."

"Why?"

His fingers flex a warning and his jaw clenches. I open the glove box.

"Look for a knife."

"Why?" I'd laugh at how petulant I sound, but I'm too angry and scared to care.

"Zero." He sighs and fixes me with a stern look. "You're really bad at this. You're the hostage. I'm the hostage-taker. You do what I say, or I hurt you. You don't ask questions. Look for a knife."

His tone is patient enough, but then he squeezes again, and an involuntary squeak escapes my mouth as his fingers dig into sensitive skin. His grip is hard enough to bruise. I move the papers around in the glove box, biting my tongue to avoid making any more incriminating noises. The pressure on my thigh relaxes.

My fingers close on a penknife, and I pull it out as the light turns green. An idea flashes in my mind, staring at the folded weapon.

"I'll crush your hand around it the minute you try to do anything." He speaks in a slow and deliberate tone, accentuating every syllable, filling them with promise. I look up to find his eyes boring into mine. I don't doubt his word for one second. A constant aura of menace and power radiates from him.

"Here," I say, holding the knife out, the immediate fear of withholding it from him overcoming the future fear of what he's going to do with it.

He shakes his head. "Not for me. For you. Cut out your tracker."

"What tracker?"

He spares a glance at me before bursting out into a loud guffaw, the sound filling the cab of the truck like a physical presence.

"'What tracker'?' Not only are you cute, Zero, you're funny too. Do you think I'm stupid? You've all got trackers."

"I don't know what you're talking about," I say, lifting my chin and trying to marshal my face into a mask of confidence.

This time he slams to a stop in the middle of the road, causing tires to screech and horns to blare behind us. The look he gives me is all the more frightening for how jovial it appears, a huge smile, white teeth contrasting with his copper beard.

"Zero, I will search every inch of your body for it. It would be my pleasure to park this hunk of junk, tear your clothing off, and start cutting some fancy designs into your beautiful skin. Where do you want my initials, on your butt? Or maybe you'd like them right across your chest?"

He twists in his seat, the index finger of his free hand reaching out, and soft as silk he slides it right under my collarbone. I'm too shocked to pull away. The light pressure of his fingertip through my blouse is obscene and provoking.

I open my mouth to attempt a protest, but his fingers squeeze my thigh again, sending a new bolt of pain and electricity up my leg. My body is reacting in embarrassing ways to his trailing finger, as if it's attached to a gentle lover, not a dangerous killer.

"You'll have to move your hand," I bite out after a few seconds of silence filled by cars still honking.

"Don't go jumping out of that window I saw you eyeballing, now," he says, turning back to the front, his glare still on me. "You'd get scuffed up real good by the road. That'd be a real shame. I'd hate to see your pretty face ruined."

I blink and look down at my lap.

The pickup accelerates and he lets go of my thigh. The coolness left behind is strange and unwelcome. "Keep your eyes on the road," I demand to hide my sudden discomfort at the situation and feeling.

"Sure thing, Zero."

I hear the grin in his voice, but don't give him the satisfaction of looking up. Taking a breath to steady myself and imagining my tub full of lavender-smelling bubbles, I tug down my slacks far enough to reveal the patch of skin the tracker is under. A tiny slice of my green panties peek out on either side of my thumb, exposing me far more than I'd like.

Prodding with my fingers until I find the rice-sized piece of technology, I place the tip of the blade against my skin and try to find my happy place. Bubbles and wine, the sound of thunder, standing in the rain.

The sharp pain zinging through me as I puncture my skin and dig out the tracker keeps me focused. A few seconds later, I'm able to stick in a fingernail and tease out my last connection to safety. Slick with blood, I pinch the tracker between two fingers, and press my palm to the cut. Using my other leg, I fold the blade back without bothering to clean it.

"Toss it out the window, Zero," he says, his eyes trained on the little patch of exposed skin.

Tugging my pants up, I press the fabric against the slice. I glare as he looks into my eyes and smirks, which tells me more in half a second than he ever could with words. A heat I'm not used to grows in my chest as I fling the tracker out the window with my last bit of hope. Now I'll need to escape by my own devices. No one's coming to get me.

The passing buildings have transitioned from the sleek skyscrapers of downtown to the more modest buildings ringed around it like the shell of a clam around a pearl. We turn onto the highway, and the wind whips across my face through the broken window, causing my hair to thrash like a dying octopus. He grabs my thigh again, trapping my fingers and interrupting my thoughts.

"Let go, you fucker," I protest, trying to tug my hand out and failing. If I can get my hand free maybe I can leave a little trail of blood out of the window.

"Now, now," he admonishes. "Can't have you dripping some of your blood out the window. I know you've got a werewolf on staff. I'm going to keep my hand right there."

A surge of anger rises and I take a swing at him. As much of a swing as I can manage across my body, anyway. My fist bounces off his bicep.

His eyebrows go up. "Was that—are you trying to punch me?"

Managing to twist somewhat, I swing again, teeth gritted. I'm not as strong as a werewolf or a golem, but I'm no weakling. His chest feels like granite.

He doesn't even flinch. "If it makes you feel better, hit away, Zero." The chuckle in his voice is even more infuriating than the grin. "It hurts my feelings, but I don't think we're at that stage of our relationship where we talk about our feelings."

"Fuck you," is all I manage, along with a few other swings. The solid thumps sound satisfying, but there's no other discernible effect. After a few tries I slump in my seat.

"All done?"

Biting back a retort, I go back to looking out the window. What on earth is wrong with me? He makes me feel like I'm seventeen, been caught drinking, and he's taking me home to ground me.

I'm sulking, my lower lip stuck out. I force my face to relax. This isn't me. I'm a respected and organized investigator. My job is to put guys like him away. Many have yelled and threatened me from the other side of the glass, and not once have I ever had trouble sleeping. I need to get my head straight before the interrogation I'm bound to be put through. I also need to be alert for any opportunity to escape. I can't let him throw me off with his sarcasm and demeaning names. I'm a fucking adult, for christ's sake.

An adult who's never been in a situation like this before. I've always been on the *other* side of the window. I don't fight, although I can hold my own. I've never felt threatened because I've never been in real danger. No one's gotten closer than the other side of the interrogation table, and even then there was someone armed nearby. Shit. I'm in way over my head.

"What are you thinking?"

"What?" I turn to him, blinking, derailed.

"You heard me." He steers us off the highway.

"We're getting off already?"

He grunts. "You didn't answer my question."

"None of your damn business." I resume my watch out of the broken window. We're barely outside of downtown, fifteen minutes from where we began.

"Thought maybe you'd want to talk. You look worried."

I roll my eyes and push back the huff of disbelief. "Of course I'm worried. I'm about to be tortured. Why would you care about me being worried?"

"Zero," he says, acting affronted. "Have I or have I not kept you from bleeding everywhere? Didn't I let you work out some frustrations with your tiny fists?"

"You knocked me out. You slapped me." I'm not sure why I find the last one more offensive.

"I had to get your attention. You were kind of pissy and I didn't have time to wait around for you to come to your senses."

"Oh, sure, that makes it perfectly valid. You're a dick." I tug my hand again, harder, trying to pull away. As I wind up to yank as hard as I can, he lets go, and the back of my hand smacks into my face. His laughter grates against every nerve I've got, and my face blooms into a slow heat from the chest up.

"Are you blushing?"

"No, I'm fucking pissed off and angry. Angry I let you out, and angry that my whole life is going to be wasted when Costecu's done with me and kills me. Or you kill me." The words fly out in a rush of fury, a squadron of bombers looking to destroy something.

He pulls into an empty parking spot on the street, turns off the vehicle, and turns to look at me. His eyes search my face. "Yeah, that's going to suck for you."

CHAPTER SIX

Druain

The look Zero is giving me is one I've seen before on countless other faces. People try to hide it—put on a brave mask, yell and posture—but I've seen it all before. She's scared. Sooner or later, they crumple, and their fear takes over. I hope she's not one of those people who get reckless when they're scared. Those people are the worst. They do stupid things, making them so much harder to protect.

Back at her base she was all fire and brimstone, but the further away from the protection of her people we get, the quicker resistance seeps out of her. I help drain it further with my tough-guy act, intimidating her as much as I can without causing any real harm. It has to be enough to keep her under control in front of Costecu so she doesn't get herself killed before I can figure out a way to get her to safety.

There must be some way.

"Stay there," I say, giving her a squeeze on the thigh as I open my door. I have to admit, there are worse thighs I could have my hand wrapped around. As I remove my hand, the quick flash of the knife slicing into her skin to remove the tracker surfaces, and I have to turn my flinch into a scowl. It'll probably scar, a small mar on her smooth skin I hate having caused. I don't want to think about her having more.

Even though I don't glance her way, I have no doubt her glare follows me as I stride around the front of the stolen pickup to collect her. I meet her gaze, solid and unwavering, as I grab the handle and pop her door open. "Come on, Zero, let's go." I hold out my hand.

She hesitates, and then her lips curve in a half smile. "Are you being chivalrous all of a sudden? Opening doors and offering hands?"

Shit. I keep doing this. Little gestures of kindness, which threaten to ruin my image. I can only shrug them off for so long before she's going to notice something serious is up. I muster my best offended face. "Zero. I'm always chivalrous. I like to give everyone the benefit of the doubt."

She snorts and rolls her eyes.

"I don't believe in three strikes, though," I add, dropping my voice into a low rumble. "Fuck up one single time and I'll be putting you through doors without opening them."

I hope my tough talk is sufficiently menacing, and I grab her wrist and tug her out of the truck with enough force to cause her to tumble a little, but not enough she'll trip. Even if she did, I'd catch her fall because I can play it off as groping. I wouldn't mind an excuse to hold her against me again, to feel the way she'd struggle against my grip.

Then again, why am I bothering to restrain myself? Evil Drew wouldn't give a crap. In fact, he'd probably have grabbed her in places worse than her waist by now. I settle for cupping her butt, giving a small squeeze as I drag her toward me. She lets out another adorable huff and paws at my shoulder, but I'm more focused on how she feels pressed to my chest. The not-insignificant thought I could throw her in the back seat and have my way with her rears up. The need to see what's hidden under her blouse has been churning in my brain ever since I got a peek at her hip and thigh.

Before I can stop myself, I grab the back of her white blouse, fingers scraping against her lower back, and tug. She spouts something in protest, but I couldn't care less. All I care about is the strips of skin and splash of color now visible through the gaps between her buttons. The swell of her breasts, the light green shade of her bra that doesn't match the deeper color of her panties—my tenuous control is strained to the limit.

We're still standing in front of the truck, and it would be so easy to toss her inside and take what I want, but that's Evil Drew thinking. I'm not him, and I won't unleash him on Zero. Instead, I spin her to face forward, pinning her hip to my thigh and letting go of her shirt, shoving down the physical pain of restraint rising in my chest.

"Stay close now, Zero," I speak over her shocked look. "This is a rough part of town. Wouldn't want anyone accosting you."

"Like you?" she mutters, a tiny growl resonating in her throat.

We're in an industrial area, but not a thriving one. Dilapidated factories from various eras line the streets. Despite appearances, some are still in use, black or white smoke oozing from various stacks. Chain-link fences attempt to keep the spread of decay out, but most have holes in them the size of trucks. Graffiti covers a good percentage of the exposed brick or concrete, most indecipherable, some rude.

I guide her along the sidewalk, making sure I'm between her and the road. A group of men, scruffy and aimless, eye us from the other side of the street, crouched like vultures in the shade of a highway overpass. I suspect the pickup we've left is in for a rough day. One steps forward onto the cracked pavement, his hand in his pocket.

"You take one more step and I'll drop you where you stand," I warn, staring at him with the easy confidence of someone who means what he says.

A pause, and then, "Meant no harm, pal."

"That's where we're different. See, Zero?" I add, turning to her as the thug melts back in with the group. "I'll deliver you to Costecu safe and sound."

She barks a laugh but says nothing else. Her arms are crossed over her chest, shoulders clenched up to her ears as close as possible, as if an arctic wind is blowing through her.

I leave her alone, give her some time to sort out her thoughts, while I sort out mine. How am I going to salvage this situation? I need to give Costecu what he wants and still get what I want out of it, which is avoiding another dead body. A not-insignificant part of me is also debating how I could get another look at her breasts. We've walked five blocks before she breaks into my detailed thoughts of all the ways I'd spend time with those soft mounds.

"Where the hell are we going?"

"You don't think I'd park our stolen truck right outside our base, did you? Do you have that low an opinion of me?"

"Yes." Her eyebrows crash together like two thunderclouds, and I suspect she would've struck me with lightning, if possible.

"You know, Zero, if we weren't on opposite sides of this thing, we would've been great friends." I chuckle.

"Why are you on Costecu's side? What are you getting out of it?"

Revenge. A silence to the screams haunting my dreams every night. "We're here."

She looks around, no doubt trying to memorize everything, find her bearings, get any information she can gather in case she can escape. Clever woman.

I knock on the unassuming metal door set in the brick wall of an old factory. I have no idea what they used to make, but it's left behind a generic shell of a building we use to cover our underground base. Costecu thinks underground is better than being exposed above ground, and in this case, I happen to agree.

A little window opens, and an eye glares at me. "Password?"

"Atracţie," I say.

"Passwords? That's your security?" Zero's sneer is pronounced and loud.

"Kinda," I reply as the heavy bolts inside slide back. The door hinges open, and I walk in first, pulling her behind me. My eyes pierce the dark inside right away, but it must take a second for hers to catch up, because she only gasps after the door clangs shut.

"This is the rest of it." I turn to our dragon. "Hey, Gil. This is the infamous Moarte."

A pointy grin spreads across his thin face, jaw elongated to a scaly snout, his bulk hidden in his dark alcove, curled up like a cat. He reaches a hand out of the gloom. While it's as big as mine, he has talons instead of fingernails.

"Ah-ah, no touching," I admonish, pulling Zero back a little. "Costecu wouldn't be happy if she's hurt before he gets to her."

Gil's face falls, the slits of his eyes narrowing a little. "Jusst a piece? Sselkie tasstes sso good."

A tapping on the concrete accompanies his shuffle forward. He doesn't get out much. It's hard to disguise his bulk and his fur. Poor Gil got the raw end of the genetic lottery. He looks fearsome and is every bit as dangerous as he looks. He likes to meet new people and then eat them.

"No, Gil. Sorry. Maybe next time." If he decides to fight me on this, it'll get messy. I tense up, shifting a bit more in front of Zero.

I'd like to enjoy her hand on my arm and her body against my back, but I can't at this moment.

"Okay, next time. I'll remember," he says after a long pause, and settles back down on his haunches.

"I won't forget," I say, stifling my sigh of relief. With a bit of planning, the next time I visit Gil it will be with someone who deserves to get eaten.

Zero's breathing and small movements behind me are distracting as I back out of the small entry room. She's clinging to me like a clam attached to a rock. After I've widened the distance past Gil's striking range, I turn and push her in front of me through the door to the next room.

"Was that a dragon?" she whispers. "I thought they were extinct."

"Not quite," is all I offer.

The next room is also dimly lit, enough so most people who come here can still see, but not too bright to offend the senses. I push the button to summon the elevator.

"After all your elevator complaints, we aren't taking the stairs?" Zero says, her false bravado betrayed by the slight tremor between the words.

"Nope. Don't want you too tired. Plus, I want to have you alone for a bit." Not sure where that came from, but I have to admit to myself, it's true. It's a little worrying I don't quite know where I end and Evil Drew begins on this subject, but both of us would like to see more of Zero.

She's got a fierceness about her, an aura of determination all the more impressive in her current situation. While it's easy for me to smell the fear, and spot the little hints of worry, not for one second has she tried to bargain for her life. The multiple attempts at escape and constant barbs thrown at me are admirable and speak of courage. I'm torn between enjoying her fire and worrying it's going to get her killed.

The elevator doesn't ding. A sudden noise like that could set off some of the more volatile members of Costecu's posse. Instead, the doors open without fanfare. No one comes out, another bit of luck.

Shepherding Zero inside, there's only one button to push, lit up a dim red color, so I push it.

"Where are we going?" she asks.

"Down." Being told she's about to meet Costecu wouldn't be beneficial, serving only to make her more nervous.

"That's so helpful," she sighs, fidgeting next to me. It's like having a restless puppy at the end of a leash, always moving even after you tell them to sit. She pokes at the wall, looks around, and opens her mouth to say something else.

"If you needed to know something, I'd tell you." It slips out of my mouth a bit harsher than I wanted, and I wish I hadn't said it, but there's no pulling it back.

"Or you could let me decide for myself. I *am* an actual adult."

Trust me, I want to tell her. *I'm going to get you out of here.*

Problem is, the *how* is still eluding me. I'm not even sure if I can. It's too dangerous to trust her to pretend in front of Costecu. She could crack the moment he lays eyes on her.

The elevator doors open to the underground complex. I pull her by the wrist straight down the hallway. No need to give anyone ideas she's anything but a captive. Our lair isn't as clean as Zero's base, not by a long shot. Slashes mark the wall, and stains mar the floors. It's so stereotypical of a lair, I cringe every time I walk down it. Would it kill someone around here to clean now and then?

A double door is at the end—a portal into the main room where Costecu organizes everything, although it might as well be an old-fashioned throne room. Costecu is a bit of a traditionalist. He's been around a while. From what I understand, he came up with the rest of the group from Wallachia.

I knock, and another little window opens. Unlike at the front door, this eye doesn't say anything to me, instead drawing back and closing the flap. Zero is fidgeting enough I could call it trembles. It might be adrenaline or fear, or perhaps both.

The big doors crack open, far enough for me to slip inside. The room is even dimmer than the hallway or the elevator. I hate all this gloom and skulking. It's such a throwback to those days hundreds of years ago when we hid in the dark like nothing more than animals. I agree with Costecu on this—hiding is not something we should do. There are better ways to go about normalizing us than conquest, and there are better ways to run a revolution than from within an underground lair. Buy some lightbulbs, at least.

Stopping fifteen feet in front of where I know Costecu will be sitting, I tug Zero back to my side, telling myself it's to show I'm in control of her.

"Ah, you've brought me my present," a voice crawls out from in front of us, a half-second before my night vision kicks in. There he is, perched in his ancient leather chair. His elbows on his knees, his eyes fixed on Zero. A vulture watching his prey, waiting for it to drop dead.

"Sir, this is Moarte."

"Hello, my dear." His words are smooth like an aged cigar.

As always, I suppress my desire to roll my eyes around him, and not only because he'd hear it and pluck them out with no effort. Besides being a fair bit older than everyone else, the major reason he's in charge in this area is because most others are as traditional as him, the kind of people who prefer letters to emails. The whole group is so regressive it hurts, but you can't argue with his results.

I nudge Zero. "You better say something," I mutter.

"Fuck you," she spits out in the direction of my boss.

A host of conflicting emotions battles for attention. Worry, anxiety, pride. Is laughter an emotion? I bottle them all up and hope he doesn't kill her on the spot. She's not going down without a fight, that's for sure.

The chair creaks as Costecu leans back, running his fingers over his leathery forehead. I hold my breath, prepared to restrain myself if he leaps up to rip her throat out. I need to keep my eye on the long game.

Instead, he emits dry laughter, a sound somewhere between sandpaper and dripping water. Something normal lungs can't make. He's never laughed before, and it sets off all my alarms.

"Well, don't you have spirit, young lady? You've certainly been a burr under my cushion for a while. It's a joy to meet you in person. What is your name so that I may address you properly?"

"Screw you."

"Oh, dear. Young people these days, no manners, hmm?" he asks the others lurking around the edges of the room. Growls and laughter follow his statement. "Please, my dear, I only wish to extend you every courtesy of my abode. No one will cause you harm."

It's a bald and blatant lie, one he can't expect her to believe. But his old-world insistence on respect, false or not, tinges everything he does.

"Go fuck yourself."

She's consistent. I suspect she's trying to provoke him on purpose. Her words are strong, but she's scooted up next to me, and she's trembling. The fact she's decided to take shelter in my shadow would be something I'd like to take time to savor, but there's no joy in this cold and dark place.

Costecu stands, unfolding like a grotesque bit of origami, all legs and arms and eyes. He steps forward, down the two steps off the platform where his chair is set. I still have my arm around Zero's waist, and she's shaking like a leaf in a tornado. The hardest thing I've ever done is not tightening my hold on her further to steady the tremors.

Costecu stalks forward until he's in front of us.

"I can smell you," he says. All the cordiality is gone from his voice, replaced by a cold flatness. His finger uncurls and he drags it down her cheek, slow as a drop of water. "Your fear. Your blood pumping through your heart."

I still my own heart, perfected through over a year of practice. I am as stone. Solid, implacable, and unmoving.

"Kiss my ass," Zero stammers, still trying.

"I've been around for far longer than you, tasty one," Costecu continues. "And I'll be around long after you're nothing but a delicious memory. Take her to a cell, Lindberg. Make sure she's comfortable, of course."

"Yes, sir," I say, and pull her away before he changes his mind.

"They're going to come rescue me," she shouts. "They're going to come get me. I'm going to lock you away forever."

I get her out the door before she can say anything else. The wood and steel make a deep sound behind us. Her breathing is ragged, her fingers fluttering against her side as she holds herself. I keep her close, and the soft movements of those fingers bounce against my ribs.

What I want to tell her is how much courage she has, and how stupid she is, and how much I want to kiss her. I satisfy myself with lowering my hand to her butt and squeezing, relishing the little yelp.

I march her down the hall, through a door, and down another hall as ugly as the last. Steps drop us further under the surface of the earth. I hope she has the presence of mind to remember this route. I'm not going all that fast, attempting to give her some time to recover and get her bearings. Another door, another set of stairs, and another hall. This one is filled with moans and cries, other prisoners in various states of interrogation and captivity.

I open a barred door, the room inside bathed in inky darkness even I can't see through. No one's around to see me being nice, and I can't bring myself to add to her problems, so I nudge her inside instead of shoving.

"Feeding is in an hour. Get some rest," I say before shutting the door. The lock turns with a clunk. Tomorrow will be here before I know it, and I need a solid plan.

The walk back to my room is filled with heavy thoughts.

CHAPTER SEVEN

Aideen

The cell is dark. Like no light has ever been down here and never will be. I shuffle around the perimeter of the room, one hand dragging across the wall. It's rough, not concrete, maybe actual carved stone. Then my toes hit something soft, and I recoil back. The possibility it's a dead body, or worse, a live one, jumps to the forefront of my mind. I've seen bodies, of course, but it's not something I enjoy being up close and personal with.

There's no grunt of protest or anger from the prone shape, so I poke it with my foot again. When it still doesn't move, I decide it's not alive. Steeling my nerves in case it's dead, I bend down and reach forward until my fingers brush cloth. I can't help the reflexive jerk away, but go back in for another poke. Rough material, something crinkly inside it. Not a body then. I breathe a sigh of relief. Cautious exploration reveals it lies along the entire length of the cell. It's a literal straw mattress for me to sleep on.

Sleeping will be difficult with the persistent sounds of people suffering around me. The door dampens them somewhat, but moans and sniffles still hover right at the edge of hearing. It's going to be impossible for me to ignore the sounds of creatures in misery.

I shuffle my feet forward now in case I bump into anything else. When my toes thunk against some kind of wood bucket in the other corner I'm less startled. I run my hand along it, and calm transforms to disgust when I figure out it's meant to be the toilet. I wipe my hand on the wall, trying to scrub away the memory of what I've just touched, but the sensation of germs skittering across my skin won't go away. My stomach clenches at the knowledge I'm about as far from a bath as I'll ever get.

The thought sends me collapsing down onto the rough bed. It puffs, and I imagine all sorts of dust, spores, and dead bugs hurtling through the air and into my lungs. Holding my head in my hands, I close my eyes even though the dark is impenetrable. I won't cry here, I won't. They'll never get that satisfaction, no matter what. I may scream in pain, beg for mercy, but I won't cry, not in front of Costecu, and certainly not in front of Lindberg.

Lindberg. There's a puzzle I want to figure out. It's something to keep my mind occupied, and I hate not understanding things. I redirect my brain to him instead of the plight I can't do anything about right now. He's not the stereotypical thug I expected from reading all the reports. Sure, he's rude, and a brute, and yes he made me cut my tracker out with an un-sanitized knife, but...he's something else too.

I got the impression while in front of Costecu he was trying to shield me. Not with his body, so much, although his arm did tense around my waist when Costecu rose. I rub the clotted slice on my hip while replaying how Lindberg's posture shifted straighter as if waiting for something, which never happened. He did the same thing in front of the dragon. It was more obvious then because he *did* push me behind him, kept the dragon away, and hurried me out of the room in quick order.

The reason for getting me away from the hungry dragon had to be more than saving me from a few scratches. I got the distinct impression that despite Costecu pretending at politeness, he wouldn't have been upset if I was missing a finger or two. His gaze seemed to go through me, as if examining my heart instead of my body. It'd felt chill and dead, like my fate was already sealed.

Restless, I get up and pace the room again, fumbling in the dark against the walls. It's not a big cell, enough for the mattress to fit along one wall of the square with no extra space on either end. Three steps along the other wall takes me to the bucket. Careful not to kick it, I'm dreading when I'll have to use it.

Back to Lindberg, who opened the SUV door for me. On the surface it seemed like he was taking control of the situation, but when I poked him about it a crack appeared in his implacable face for a split second. Then he'd pulled me out, but it was strange, forced, and not even close to what he could have done if he'd been truly angry. I'm sure it's a coincidence. Why would he go easy on me? There's no reason I can think of.

The door under my fingertips is petrified wood. Where did they get lumber this old, and why is it not bars? It's like being in dungeon of a castle. I wish there was any bit of light so I could ground myself. As it is, it's like floating in space, except I'm on the floor. I have to keep counting my steps for fear of walking into a wall.

I sit on the crappy excuse for a bed again, and with nothing else to do in this dank cell, replay the past hours searching for inconsistency. Lindberg slapped me after knocking me out, then dragged me by my throat right through the lobby. What would have happened if I'd refused to cooperate? Would he have broken my fingers? Now I'm not protected by adrenaline, those moments bring queasiness to my stomach.

My hands are shaking, and I roll onto my side, facing a wall I can't see.

I can't believe I said those things to Lindberg and Costecu. I wish he had killed me right then, to spare me what's to come, but the thought of everything ending is frightening. I have no doubt everything is going to end, one way or another, and I'd like to think I have the strength to make it on my terms. Advancing my own demise goes against all my survival instincts, though. I want to hope against everything there's some way I can escape.

There has to be a way out of here. Lindberg escaped from us, so I can escape from him. I'm smarter than he is. Maybe he'll do something stupid, like I did. I hate the phrase, but we're all "human." Everyone makes mistakes. The one I made was extra stupid, and I still don't understand why I did it. Whatever possessed me to go in there alone has long since faded, and now all I feel is shame.

I ball my fists and push the thought away. I won't give up. Lindberg's right when he said I need to rest, or at least try. I can't be tired or out of sorts. They could let me rot for days, weeks, before doing something. I need to be rested, and I need a plan for when they come for me. Preparation is the best defense against desperation.

Sleep doesn't come to me, though. The mattress isn't what I'd call adequate, never mind luxurious. As soon as I push one stalk down, another one pokes me through the thin fabric. The jacket and slacks I'm wearing aren't made for sleeping. My flats pinch, but I'd rather die than walk on this floor barefoot.

My unsuccessful attempt at sleep is interrupted by a clanking. Jerking upright, ready for anything to happen, I steel myself for hands or worse. Instead, another clatter rocks through the air, and then silence. I'm tensed for any sort of hint as to what's happened, but the only thing in the air are those omnipresent whimpers of the other captives.

Something rotten assails my nostrils. I sling my arm across my nose, and remember what Lindberg said earlier about feeding. It must be food shoved through the hatch in the door, although based on the smell that's a loose interpretation of the word. Scooting to the side of the pallet closest to the door, I test the darkness with my hand, searching for the plate or bowl of whatever they've given me.

My fingertips brush something smooth and cool, and jerk back. Steeling myself and probing again, I find the lip, a curved edge. Dragging the bowl across the floor, the sounds of metal clang and ring against stone. Why would they give me something metal? Maybe this is the mistake I was hoping for.

Then I make a mistake by poking my fingers into the bowl to touch what's in it. I wrinkle my nose and bring my fingers up to sniff. Slimy, warm, and not any better smelling up close. The distinct smell of blood and organs assaults me. It's awful, and my throat closes as I try not to retch. There's no way I'm eating it, whatever "it" is.

Holding it out at arm's length, I take the two steps needed to dump it in the bathroom bucket, then return to the bed with the empty but still stinky bowl. Maybe I can use it to make a weapon. Twisting, pulling, I strain my muscles in an attempt to flatten the bowl so I can use it to dig or stab, but it's thick and unmoving.

The smell is worse than the moans. It's filling the room like a toxic cloud of miasma. I'll have to burn these clothes when I get out of here.

I can't help but laugh to myself, then I bite my tongue. There will be no laughing at the notion of escape. I will get out of here, whatever it takes. Lying back on the pricks of the straw, dim, colored swirls dance in front of my eyes. My brain is desperate to focus on anything, even if it has to make something up.

Lindberg shoulders his way into my mind again. Huge and solid. Beardy. Strong. Always threatening, but never hurting. Okay, he slapped me, more than once, but I can't imagine it was hard from his perspective. He could take my head off if he wanted. He didn't break any fingers, although he had good excuses to do it, and he didn't cut my tracker out, he made me cut it out. I stop rubbing the scab on my hip, not sure when I started.

The stare he gave me when my hip was exposed almost made me shiver, even though his eyes were spitting fire hot enough to melt flesh. It felt as if I'd shown him everything, yet he was hungry for more, those few bare inches of skin a mere snack. Those moments replay over and over in my mind, and I shift on the mattress, ill at ease, unwilling to stop thinking about it, but uncomfortable with how it makes me feel.

I've always been cautious, steady, and risk-averse in my job and my personal life. The few times in recent memory when I've dated, it's always been with men who were similar. Not that I want to date Lindberg, far from it, but his brand of fire and intensity makes me want to do other things with him, and that scares me. Instead of warning me away like it should, fear is triggering an urge to experience more. *What the hell is wrong with me?*

I roll onto my stomach. The straw crackles. Thoughts of how filthy it must be makes my skin crawl. I'm sure it's never seen soap and water. Who even knows who was in here last and how much they drooled on it, or bled on it, or worse. It's even a little damp, something I'd managed to ignore up to this point. Being underground means not only is everything cold, but there's a slight sheen of water everywhere. If it weren't for the mystery food in the crap bucket, I bet I'd be smelling mildew.

I wish for my tub. Hot water, some nice bubbles, maybe lavender or lemongrass scented. Maybe both, one from the bubbles and one from candles, calming but warm. A nice glass of wine, a Tempranillo, or something mild. I'd like to say I'd pick something less stereotypical than ocean and thunderstorm sounds to listen to, but that would be a lie. Thunderstorms are amazing. The sound, the way the lightning arcs across the sky, and of course the rain. Fat, heavy drops, tumbling out of the sky to splash on my upturned face. I'd never admit it to anyone, but a few times I've gone somewhere remote so I could get naked in the rain. It not only feels amazing, it does wonderful things for my skin.

A high-pitched keening sound breaks me out of my reverie. It's thin and plaintive, and the hot bath and rain disappears in a puff of fear. The sound trails off to nothing. There's no reaction from any of the other moaners.

The cold I'd been ignoring seeps into my skin. The adrenaline I thought had worn off before is now ebbing to a new low. My hip throbs, my throat is scratchy as if I've been screaming, the wrist Lindberg dragged me around by is a little sore, and there's a dull ache in the muscles of my ass. That must be where he'd grabbed and dug his fingers in. It's like everywhere he touches I get bruises.

Flexing my wrist around, testing how sore it is, most of the tension goes away with the stretching. Then I test the ache in my butt. It's much more tender, but I can't stop prodding, exploring the extent of it. In some strange way it feels good. Dull and deep, spreading along nerves lighting up with every touch. It's like wiggling a loose tooth or rubbing a sore muscle, strangely addictive.

I'm not sure how long I poke, but tiredness is winning. I spare a moment to recognize the chill in the air. I've never been bothered by the cold before, so the chill creeping up my limbs must be from the lack of sleep, and emotions I refuse to acknowledge. It would take a lot lower temperature than this to do more than inconvenience me, but the knowledge doesn't help me feel better.

Having my eyes open or closed makes no difference in visibility, but I must've slept at some point because I wake up from a dream. The dream washes out of my mind as I blink to try to clear the ever-present darkness.

The images were of Lindberg, of all people. His face shoved in mine, telling me he's taking me away. Where, he doesn't say. Instead he's grabbing my wrist and pulling. I tug back, and in response he picks me up and tosses me over his shoulder as if I were a small sack of potatoes. I pound my fists into his back, but he laughs and called me "tiny-fist," says he hopes I'm "having fun."

Confused memories follow, blurry remembrances of a room springing up from the ground wall by wall. The room is dim, not dark like in the cell, but the type of dark caused by curtains over windows. Sparkling motes fall through a shaft of light. The floor is carpet, a thick pile that would be hell to vacuum. A chair rests in the middle of it all, with Lindberg sitting in it. He's waiting for me to do something, expecting something from me, but what it is I can't figure out.

"What do you want?" I screamed at him, but he only looked at me, face unmoving, eyes blazing into mine, hands resting on his knees.

"Stop staring. Stop looking at me. Tell me what you want." No amount of screaming did anything. I kept at it though, yelling at him, cursing, dredging up every obscure epithet I could remember.

When my voice was hoarse and I couldn't utter one more word, he stood, a leviathan rising from the depths. I fell to my knees on the soft carpet, digging fingers into the red pile.

"All done?" he'd said.

I could only nod, helpless, unable to do anything but accept my fate. Whatever he wanted to do, I had no energy to stop him. He'd strode over, and as his hand was reaching out to touch me, I woke up.

The dream scatters like petals ripped from flowers in a windstorm, whipping through my mind. The darkness is my only companion, not Lindberg, and not my bath. I'd welcome either of them at this point. It hasn't even been a day and I'm already having nightmares about him, cut off in this horrible cell and waiting for death or worse.

Maybe I should go crazy and get it over with. I experiment with a low moan, joining in the small chorus of others, feel ridiculous within seconds, and shut my mouth.

I touch my ass again, searching for the ache from yesterday, not sure why I have this strange urge to feel the reminder of Lindberg. It's still sore, but less so. My fingers find a perfect spot, and the zing of nerves curves up my spine in a way that's pleasing, though it shouldn't be. I push a few more times, but the zing is less each time as the nerves acclimate, leaving me feeling cold.

I've been reduced to poking my own butt to feel something. I'm going crazy. I want him to grab me again so I can get a new bruise to explore. Every rational part of me screams in protest.

I sigh and roll onto my back. This is boring. I get why people who are in prison are super ripped. What else is there to do?

There's enough room for me to stretch out and do push-ups. Twenty. Thirty-five sit-ups. Okay, that killed a few minutes. I try wall squats, but the stones of the wall aren't regular, and it's not particularly comfortable. I laugh to myself.

"What do you want, a padded wall?" I ask out loud. My own voice startles me, ears already used to muffled moans and groans. I should've been talking earlier. It brings a feeling of normality to this situation.

"Okay, what else do I know? Lunges? Is there enough room?"

There is, to my secret chagrin. I hate lunges. I force myself through them, and then start to wrack my brain for any other exercises I can do.

There's nothing else to do but wait.

CHAPTER EIGHT

Druain

Waking up from a fitful rest, the type where you can't decide if you were awake or asleep, the scraps of dreams that could've been nightmares flutter away.

Costecu wouldn't interrogate Zero for a few hours, wanting to let her stew, and there was nothing constructive I could do until then, so I'd wandered to the kitchen to see what she'd be given to eat. Offal, organs, and entrails ripped from unfortunate creatures, same as every other day, no matter who's locked up. Somehow, I don't think selkies eat raw meat. If I could do anything to change what she got, I would have, but Mather is protective of his "food" and his bites hurt.

After ending up in my room, I'd paced a few minutes, my brain unhappy with my inactivity, but my common sense made me stay put. I'd only mess everything up if I tried anything, but even with the logic it was difficult not to do something rash.

Watching Costecu touch her triggered a rage in me I haven't felt in a long time. He hasn't done anything to deserve such an honor. As much as I've put her through, I haven't been creepy. Okay, so there was ass grabbing, clothes pulling, maybe a kiss or two. Somehow, that's not as weird as a single finger across her cheek. I earned my liberties by getting her out of their base and all the way here without hurting anyone else, even though I could have. It would have been so easy to let Gil have a taste, and Costecu wouldn't have minded too much.

Or maybe I'm making excuses and rationalizing my behavior. Evil Drew is smirking at me, not regretting for one instant any of the gropes and grabs. Am I as bad as Costecu?

I roll out of my bed and stretch, reaching up to brush my fingers against the rough ceiling stones, avoiding the one bare lightbulb hanging down. Costecu tried to build a medieval castle underground to remind himself of the old world. I'd take the sterile concrete and bright fluorescents of Zero's headquarters over this dank and musty abomination.

Something everyone here has in common is a fear of the modern world. Costecu could have bought a building with all the wealth he's accumulated over the ages. We could have a cafe, telephones, windows. I'd be able to drive a nice company car, drink coffee in the mornings, and waste time on the internet like every other human working a job. Instead, we get a base carved under an abandoned factory, with bare wires lining the walls to bring power to this lair. Just because I have to go and beat people up doesn't mean I want to live in the dark ages.

Costecu misses the power he had back then. Hiding in the background, but pulling all the strings. Now he's sour he can't manipulate the world anymore because humans have taken control of their own destinies. Communication helped—radio, TV, the internet. He's grasping to get his control back and attempting to recreate the past however he can.

Turning to make my bed, I sift through the half-dreams to find the relevant pieces of a plan I'd been formulating before I'd dozed off. It's a puzzle still missing the center. Maybe it's not the best idea, but it's all I can think of so I'll make it work.

Sitting down on the smooth sheets, rumpling them again, I take a few breaths to calm down and center myself. If I'm going to pull this off, I need to be steady. Costecu can't suspect a thing, the old bastard. I'm sure I can pull it off, but it means bad times ahead for Zero until I can get her to the safety of my cabin.

I've never been much of a woodsman, instead preferring either the city with the bustle of people, or a nice natural cave, so I tend to forget about the cabin. I say "my" cabin, but it's not really mine. I came into possession of it after the previous owner ceased needing to use it because I killed him. That death doesn't weigh on me much. He was a nasty wight, overstepping his bounds and making the news before Costecu was ready. His kills weren't hidden well enough. He was a lot stronger than I'd expected from his thin limbs, but nothing a little bonfire in the woods behind the cabin couldn't solve. I'd rate it the third worst-smelling creature I've burned to death.

I never took anyone else when I managed to get away to the cabin, either because I forgot or they weren't important enough to risk compromising it. I've been keeping it for a rainy day, and this might be it. An hour's drive west of the city, and then another thirty minutes along a little two-lane highway. Remote and hard to find, which is a good thing and a bad thing. She'd never find it on her own, but Costecu doesn't know about it either.

If he embraced technology at all, the cellphone in my pocket could lead him right to me, her, and the cabin, but he doesn't. I keep the phone, even though having it on me would get me in trouble. Even I can't resist a mindless game sometimes. With no way for a signal to penetrate underground, that's all it's good for anyway.

First things first. I have to get Zero out of here without tying the escape to me, and with enough head start they won't notice. Since I know what I'm going to do, it's tempting to go down and let her loose, but Costecu's not going to wait much longer to interrogate her. He likes to play with his new toys, even though he pretends patience. As horrible as it'll be, I should wait until after his first round of questioning. If she doesn't crack, he'll let her sit for a few days, which would be a nice buffer for her to get away before he realizes it.

I don't *want* to be anywhere nearby when he's questioning her, because it's going to be painful to watch, but I don't have a choice. I'd been "encouraged" to sit in on one of his interrogations once, and it was not enjoyable. The casual violence I employ is one thing, but premeditated and deliberate pain is a different beast. I'd also never dream of restraining someone so they can't defend themselves. That's cowardice. I fight fair, while Costecu seems to enjoy preying upon people who can't help themselves. If I had to watch him pick Zero apart while she's strapped to a chair I'd lose my damn mind.

On the other hand, the thought of leaving her alone with him is abhorrent. I've never cared about this before, but then I've never helped capture anyone who wasn't an idiot or deviant. Zero isn't an idiot, and while she might be a deviant in ways I'm determined to find out about, she doesn't eat babies or collect people.

The personalized way I took her also sticks in my mind. From the moment she walked in with those green eyes and cocky attitude,

I haven't been able to scrub away my guilt or my fantasies. She's my responsibility. I'm the one who took her, and I'm the one who will take her away to safety.

Still, I find it hard to leave my room. I pause, not remembering when I got off the bed to pace. I need to look at the big picture. This torture is going to happen, whether I want it to or not, so it may as well be me in control. This isn't the time to get cold feet because it makes me uncomfortable. It's never stopped me before, and I'm not about to let it now.

Out the door of my room, I trace the path back to Costecu's "throne room." I hesitate only a moment in front of the heavy doors before knocking for entry. Before they can creak open all the way I push inside and march up to Costecu in his chair.

"Let me be the one to question her," I say, the full force of my most commanding voice booming forth and echoing around the room.

Costecu looks up at me from his book and steeples his fingers. "This is interesting. You've never asked before."

It's a statement, but the implied question is why I'm doing something out of character. "I brought her in. I've spent some time with her. It's important for you to get as much information out of her as possible, and I understand her."

He stares at me, unblinking, and I stare right back. The whole not-needing-to-blink thing undead have going on has always put me off. Don't their eyes dry out? I keep myself still, don't shift, don't fidget, don't move. Let him try to glean something. I'm confident and nobody's going to intimidate me.

"Why?" He asks the question, bald and blatant.

"I can get you what you need. You saw her. She's got a spark of resistance, but I know how to get to her." This is all true. I'll call her "girl," or "honey," and she'll be so pissed she'll tell me anything.

"You could tell me her triggers."

He's being pushy, testing me in a way he thinks is sly. He's right I've never asked, so he's probably testing me to see if there are other motives.

"Sure, if you want to waste your time and energy. You'll have to spend hours getting the type of rapport I already have with her. But, hey, if you want to screw around, you're the boss." It's a risky tactic, but it should appeal to his practical side, or at least his desire not to be seen as frivolous.

Another few leaden seconds tick by as he keeps staring at me. "Fine. If you think you can, you are free to try. However, I shall watch, and if you make no progress, then I'll be forced to step in."

I expected him to want to watch, but it doesn't mean I like it. I was hoping he wouldn't care as much if it weren't him doing the torturing, but like I said, he likes to play with his new toys.

"Fine. I'm going to get her now."

"I shall be down shortly. Do wait for me. Take Georg with you."

Shit. I wasn't expecting an escort. I was hoping I'd have a few minutes to explain what was going on, so she'd at least be prepared, but that's not going to work. Evil Drew chuckles, and reminds me it will be more authentic this way, and less dangerous to the plan. He's also looking forward to groping her again.

I spin around and stride out, brain boiling with plans and counterplans and what-ifs enough to make steam come out of my ears. I slow from a stride to an amble, giving me extra minutes to think this over and decide what I'll do if this all goes bad.

Georg glides after me, footsteps on the edge of my hearing. Costecu's left-hand man of his left-hand man. High enough up the hierarchy he thinks he's all that, but too craven to get much further. He tries to model himself in Costecu's image, but he's easily intimidated. Easy for me, anyway. He tried to threaten me when I started rising the ranks, and it did not go well for him. By the time I was done breaking his fingers, he'd figured out vampires don't intimidate me.

Stopping before we get to her door, I turn to him and stick a finger in his chest, hard. "Don't fuck with her, don't touch her, don't even think about biting her. This is my prisoner. My responsibility. If you do something to piss me off, it's going to piss off Costecu, and then I'll stake you into dust so fast you'll travel back in time, where you'll find me, ready to stake you *again*."

It sounded better in my head, but he takes a step back anyway. Tone of voice does more than words do. I turn and stalk the remaining few feet, turn the lock, and open her door. I can't help what comes out of my mouth next.

"Let's talk."

The words have barely left my lips before she's flying at me, arm cocked back. A quick step to the side and she's flying past me, stopped only when reaching the end of my arms because I've grabbed her around the waist.

"Whoa, there, Zero. No need for that."

She manages to twist and clonk me upside the head with a metal bowl.

"Okay, now that hurt," I growl, rip the bowl out of her hand, and toss it back into the cell. It crashes to the floor, making a metallic wobbling noise as it spins down. I stare at her the whole time, and she stares back until the sound has ceased.

"Fuck you," she says through clenched teeth.

"Hopefully soon. Let's not rush things." I toss her over my shoulder, biting back a smug smile. Been thinking about doing this since I hauled her away the first time. She struggles in a satisfying way, fists beating against my back like a drum, but my arm around her thighs keeps her clamped to me. I stroll toward the interrogation rooms.

"Piece of shit," she keeps yelling. "Put me down, you fucking douchebag. I know how to walk."

"Someone's cranky. You lost walking privileges when you tried to hit me. Play nice, and things will be a lot easier for you."

"Scre—" she pauses. "I mean, suck a dick."

"That's more your specialty, isn't it?"

The noise she makes is so filled with rage it almost has substance, some sort of cross between a cat in heat and a honey badger going through a woodchipper.

"I'd bite it off."

"You know, I think you would. Don't worry, I'm traditional. This is only our second date. I believe in waiting until at least the fifth one for oral sex."

"If you think I'd let your filthy mouth anywhere near me—"

"Zero, if I wanted to, you couldn't stop me."

"Fucking misogynistic prick."

I tune out the rest of her admirable and creative swearing as we approach my destination. Georg hasn't said a peep the whole time while trailing behind us. I kind of wish he would try something. I'd lay money Zero would come out the victor.

Pushing open the door to the interrogation room, I flick on the light. The bare bulb floods out a sharp white glare, designed to be uncomfortable for most of the potential occupants. I toss Zero down onto the wooden chair. It's not metal, because even metal wouldn't be as strong as this ancient thing. It's thick, heavy, and with so many layers of varnish and age you could smash it over a troll's' head and the chair would win.

Rings on each leg chain it to the floor. It can move a little, but it's not going anywhere. Holding Zero down with one hand, I strap her wrists to the chair's arms with leather bands. One for each forearm and one for each calf. She tries to fight, but I could overpower her in my sleep.

"Let me go," she shouts with an edge of desperation.

"No can do, Zero. You sit tight for a minute or two. I'll be right back."

Shooing Georg out of the room in front of me, I close the door and move around the corner to the observation room. There's no two-way glass here, but instead a metal shutter I raise. Bars block off any attempt at escape. It's a primitive way to view a primitive custom.

"Hi, there. Costecu will be here shortly. He wants to watch." I wave to her cheerfully, and she growls something incoherent. Her fingers are gripping the front of the chair's arms, knuckles white as they hold on for dear life.

The pity and regret brewing in my gut over what's about to happen is dangerous. I take a deep breath and shove the feelings down, saving them for contemplation later. If I'm going to do this, I can't be conflicted. This might be the hardest thing I've done in recent memory, but it'll be over soon enough, like all the other things I've done, I try not to remember.

She pulls at the restraints and rocks the chair back and forth. I keep my mouth shut and give her respect for trying. Georg skulks next to me, a small grin on his face. Someday I'm going to stake him. That'll be a good day.

Someone clears their throat, and I turn around to find Costecu already seated in one of the viewing chairs. I always forget how quiet the bastard is. He can sneak up on a mouse.

"Are we all ready?" he says, voice smooth as quicksilver.

"Yup." As I walk back into the room with her, she's staring between the bars at Costecu.

"You won't win," she says to him. Her voice is steady and low. In the face of terrible things, some people tend to lose all fear, because everything they're scared of has already happened.

With an easy movement, I take her left pinky and snap it backwards. The crack is quiet, but her scream is not, and it's going to echo in my skull longer than it does across the stones.

"Now, now, Zero. Don't speak unless spoken to. There's a good girl. Ignore him. Focus on me and what I'm saying."

I turn so Costecu can't see my face, look down at her, and concentrate with all my might to give her as much strength as I can. *This will all be over soon, Zero.*

CHAPTER NINE

Aideen

Unable to look away from my pinky, held against the back of my hand at an unnatural angle, my stomach churns. Hot, sharp pain shoots along the side of my hand. I'm screaming and I can't stop.

With a final gasp of air, my lungs stop pushing out noise, but my mouth still hangs open.

Lindberg is staring down at me, intense eyes burning through my skull. He's not smiling. In fact, his face is verging on anger, brows furrowed and mouth twisted in a frown. It doesn't look like he's enjoying this, which throws me for a loop, but maybe this is his happy face.

All these thoughts help to distract me from the throbbing yet sharp pain radiating from my hand. Burning and icy chill assault my nerves all at once. Adrenaline is gushing through my body to help dull the pain, but only more torture is coming. It's not going to be enough.

"Tell me your name," Lindberg says. An easy request, but I'm caught off guard. With all the intense hours I've spent with him, it feels like he should already know it.

If I tell him, is that giving in already? How long do I hold out a small bit of information? However, if I do cave it sets a dangerous precedent: he can get information out of me with little effort, and then he'll have no reason to kill me. If I'm stubborn and difficult, they might give up, and I won't have to be strapped to this chair for however many sessions it takes.

"Zero," I force out of my throat with a sneer. "Isn't that right?"

He smiles, his eyes crinkling a little at the corners. "No. That's what my name for you is. I can see how you'd get confused, but what do your friends call you?" He leans down, his face hovering over mine, his large hand resting over mine. The dull throb kicks into high gear as he tweaks my broken finger.

I can't help the scream, but I manage to strangle it short by clamping my jaw shut.

"I really don't want to break more of your fingers," he growls to me, voice low and menacing. He brushes my cheek with a knuckle, and wetness smudges with it. The tenderness of the move contradicts his tone in every way, which only serves to confuse. Maybe that's the point. "All I'm asking is your name."

My chest tightens and I spit in his face. The response is instant. My ring finger is snapped backward with a sickening pop and I squeeze my eyes shut. The pain follows an instant later, jagged electricity up my wrist and forearm. I'm screaming again. Sweat forms on my face, a thin layer of damp crawling toward my eyes.

Over my heavy breathing he speaks again.

"It's only a name. If you're worried I'll start calling you by your proper name, then don't. You'll always be Zero to me. I want to build a rapport, you know? You and me, together. No secrets."

His touch across my jaw is rough. I feel callouses slide over my skin, his pinky coming to rest under my ear. I clamp my jaw and refuse to react, but as the tension in my shoulders reaches a breaking point, the hand disappears. I lift my head to see him standing a pace in front of me, his bulk blocking my view of Costecu through the bars.

"No."

He sighs and steps forward again, his hand once more resting over mine. He nudges my broken fingers, causing another spike of electricity to jolt across my hand. Shouldn't it go numb at some point?

"Tell me your name. I promise it's not worth fighting over."

"No," I whisper.

"You're going to tell me. I don't want to hurt you."

His face softens, or maybe I'm imagining it. It's hard to tell, because my vision is blurry. My heart is racing. He has a point. Maybe I should tell him and get it over with.

No. I can't give in, no matter what I want, or what I think I want. I'm confused, in pain, and I can't trust myself. Easier to keep refusing than try to figure out what I should and shouldn't say. I want to tell him.

"Zero," I say, tongue snaking out to taste a salty tear that's snuck into the corner of my lips.

He clenches his jaw, and I expect my next finger to break, closing my eyes and sinking my chin down in preparation. Instead, his hand leaves mine and I hear him take a step back. Nothing else happens, and I wait, counting in my head in time with the throbbing in my fingers. After a minute I open my eyes enough to peek through my matted lashes to find him standing and staring at me.

"I wish you'd've told me," he says, turning and reaching through the bars to a table on the other side. His hand comes back with a pair of pliers and a roll of gauze.

He kneels in front of me, and as soon as his hand touches my shoe, a flash of intuition tears into my brain. "No, no, no, no," I whine, unable to help myself, twitching my foot around as much as I can in the tight restraint, struggling and tugging.

It's no use. He pulls my flat off with ease, and then grabs my bare foot. His thumb wraps around the arch of my foot, his fingers across the top, and they clamp down hard. I might as well try to pull my captured appendage out of granite.

"Last chance," he says, working the tip of the pliers under the nail of my middle toe. The cold metal digging into my skin is already painful. A pressure at the base of the nail is a dire warning of what's to come.

I run my tongue over my lips, trying to spread some moisture over the dry skin, but there's none left. This can only be the beginning, and already I'm exhausted and wired all at the same time. What would be the harm in giving in?

"My name is Zero." The tremble in my voice is unavoidable.

Lindberg's eyes don't leave mine as his bicep tenses and he pulls.

It's not sharp, nor is it fast. My toenail being yanked out is a slow and burning sensation, like it's been lit on fire and smashed with a hammer, stretched over what must be only a few agonizing seconds.

I can't stop this scream, tearing from my throat and forcing my head back. Eyes that won't close stare at the ceiling. I breathe in to scream again, tears rolling down my face. I can't tell if he's done or not. My world has been reduced down to white-hot agony, a pounding of shrieking intensity. A pressure closes around my throbbing digit, squeezing tight and adding to the pain. My head falls forward, all the tense muscles collapsing at once. Through my watery vision I can barely make out him wrapping some gauze around my toe, and he's holding it tight in his hand.

"Can't have you getting an infection," he says, his words dim and fuzzy through my pounding ears. "What's your name?"

"Aideen Duffy." I try to keep the words in between the huge breaths wracking my chest, but my lungs betray me. I can't imagine a worse pain and would rather get shot than endure it again. It might hurt more, but at least it would be over. I try to remember my resolutions before all this started, but my memories are scrambled.

What was I supposed to do? In between wishing he'd cut off my foot, I remember: piss him off so maybe he'll kill me fast. The smallest hope I'd carried of escaping hasn't survived the flames of this torture. I'm not getting out of this.

"Was that so hard?" he asks from where he's kneeling, hand still holding the gauze around me. Then he tears off a strip of tape, fastens it tight around my toe, and stands. "Now. Tell me what you know about us."

My eyes follow him as he walks back to the bars to reach through onto the table and sets the pliers down. It's a small comfort. "I know you're the scum of the earth," I say, my voice cracking.

He turns to stand in front of me, once again filling my entire vision. I drop my chin to my chest and close my eyes. It's the only way I can exert any control, which only makes the throbbing of my toe worse. It's taken my mind off my broken fingers, although they're still fighting for attention. His fingers grab my chin and pull my head up, but I squeeze my eyes tighter.

"Not looking at me won't make this go away," he says, voice flat. It doesn't sound like he's pissed off in the slightest. I need to try harder.

"Suck a dick."

"Zero, are you trying to make me angry?" His voice is not the low growl I fear and want, but a rumbling chuckle. I open my eyes to find a smile hovering under his beard.

"Yes," I admit. The throbbing isn't going away, and it's making it hard to think. Shouldn't adrenaline be dulling the pain by now?

The fact this may be duller than it should be isn't something I want to dwell on.

"Now why would you do that?" He bends down a little closer, his face hovering maybe a foot from mine, his eyes flicking back and forth, looking for...what?

"Because, fuck you," I manage to spit out, underscoring my words with a glare. "Bite me," I add for good measure.

He makes a noise that's a cross between laughter and surprise. I can't find the energy in myself to get upset anymore. Let him make fun of me, let him think I'm being silly. He can look down on me and demean me all he wants, but I still have my pride, and my determination. I can still do something.

"Suck a dick," I say, taking advantage of his continued silence.

He chuckles and reaches out. I flinch away from his large hand as it reaches toward me again, but I can't get away as he tucks a damp strand of hair behind my ear. "Repeating yourself already? Try all you want, you won't be making me mad."

"Go ahead, kill me and get it over with," I reply before I can stop myself. "I'm not going to tell you anything, you fucking piece of garbage."

His eyebrows raise like thunderclouds. "You've already told me your name, Zero." The accent he places on the name he gave me is strong. "It only took two fingers and a toenail. I figure by the time we get to breaking your kneecaps, you'll be telling me about the birthmark on your cute little bottom."

His condescension is all the worse for the situation I'm in. I can't even mount a proper protest, because my toe has moved from agony to literal fire. The pounding feels like my heart has moved down there and is beating to get out. Each thump sends a new wave of pain up my foot, tentacles of ache spreading through my veins. Even still, I'm finding it hard to keep my eyes open. Alternate waves of exhaustion and energy are fighting for the upper hand.

He taps me on the cheek. "Stay awake there, Zero. No passing out yet. We've just started."

"Eat shit."

"Not most days." He turns back to the table and something scrapes before I catch a glint of metal in his hand. As he moves I can see it's a small knife.

"Can't handle me yourself, huh?" I ask, desperate and aggressive. "Gotta use a knife to get me to talk, huh? Too squeamish to do it with your bare hands, or somethin'? Big, strong Lindberg, scared to hit a girl?"

He pauses, and for an instant I see another one of those nasty grins, but then his face twists into rage. He leans forward in one violent movement, shoving his face into mine.

"Don't fuck with me, Zero. You have no idea what you've gotten yourself into."

Maybe I've hit a nerve. He seemed to hit his anger switch quick. I should keep trying. If I wasn't already in incredible pain, he would be scary, but how much worse can it get?

"I know exactly what I've gotten myself into. A big, dumb dwarf taking orders from some old-as-fuck vampire. A lapdog. He says bark, you say woof."

The knife comes slashing down and thuds into the chair next to my forearm. It twinges and shudders, buried a good three inches into the hardwood.

"I'm nobody's lapdog," Lindberg growls.

"Woof," I bark, then cough as another blast of heat shoots up from my foot. "Doggie gonna bite me?"

My cheek stings and I'm looking at the wall of the room. The delayed realization he's slapped me catches up to my brain at the same time the hot pain blossoms across my face. My ear rings.

"A slap?" I croak. The taste of blood trickles onto my tongue from somewhere. "What are you, a child?"

This time I black out for a split second as the back of his hand comes around and snaps my head the other way. The cheek is swelling already, and it's hot. Hotter than when he slapped me when he first captured me ages ago. The thought he must've been holding back scares me a little, but I won't have to be scared much longer. He's bound to snap soon, and then I can rest.

"Anything else?" he asks. His voice seems too calm for the situation, but I can't be bothered to wonder, and I don't care.

"At least you're using your own hands now," I mumble around my now puffy lip. "Maybe you should ask for a doggie treat."

He lunges, and then his hand is around my throat. I've got one more chance to piss him off before he chokes me into unconsciousness, one more shot to try to seal my fate and goad him into going all the way. Calmness settles over me. I won't have to worry about paperwork or tracking down people like him. Or budgets, or how many people I couldn't save today, or if I'm drinking too much coffee. I'll miss my baths, but I won't miss status meetings.

"Fucking do it. Prove you're a man, and not a dog. You'll feel really awesome knowing you killed a woman strapped to a chair. I bet your dick will get real hard thinking about it tonight."

I don't even notice him squeeze as everything fades to black a lot quicker than I expected. My toe fades, my fingers fade, my face fades, and the last thing I see are his eyes, glowing and burning into me.

CHAPTER TEN

Druain

Clever woman. I should have thought of that angle first. Pretending to get pissed off at her and knocking her out to end the session. I have to give her props, though. She can't know I'm on her side, so she was really trying to get me to kill her. I'm not an amateur, and it wouldn't have worked, but it was a good excuse to choke her. A few seconds of pressure on the large artery feeding her brain, and she blacked out. Everyone does.

As I take a moment to stare at her limp body in the chair, making sure she's still breathing, Costecu shouts at me. He doesn't shout often.

"Idiot."

He's also not so direct all that often.

"Whoops," I say, trying to remain casual. If I don't make a big deal out of it, maybe he'll calm down.

"Wake her up," he commands from the other side of the bars. If I'd killed her he would have heard her heart stop, and he'd be much angrier. The twin disappointments of denying him a plaything and the information she's got in her brain would send him over the edge.

"Not sure that's a good idea," I reply, undoing the straps holding her to the chair. I need to get her back to her cell before she wakes up. I'd be happy to get her out of this room before she wakes up. Stay sleeping, Zero.

"We've barely started. I didn't come down here for nothing."

"I told you, she's tougher than she looks. This was a little introduction." I undo her ankles, careful not to touch her toe. A touch of red is seeping through the gauze. It's going to get infected in a filthy place like this unless I clean it. I'll need to go to the infirmary. If her toe turned green and fell off, she'd be pretty pissed.

"How could you let her anger you so, Druain?" His voice has calmed somewhat, but it's the calm before a hurricane.

"Guess I should have taken a nap. Must be tired." It's a thin excuse, and I'm treading close to the line between Evil Drew and me. I've got to get her out of here before the inconsistencies add up. I toss her over my shoulder, paying attention to the hand with the broken fingers. "I'll get her back in her cell and we'll try again tomorrow."

Bustling out, using every ounce of confidence and I-know-what-I'm-doing swagger, I leave Costecu sputtering behind me. As old and commanding as he is, even he's never been able to stop me when I make up my mind about something. It took a bit of work, but I've got his subconscious trained to let me go when I want to go.

Costecu is berating Georg in place of me, something I'm thankful for as I swerve and change course away from the cells. According to my inner clock, which is seldom wrong, it's a bit after six in the evening. The shift will be changing, and there won't be a lot of people there to question me.

I luck out. The only one in the infirmary is Dr. Emeris, an old and deliberate creature. I'm not really sure what he is, to be honest. He's excellent at surgery, on both alive and dead subjects, whether they want it or not, and he has a strange collection of medical grotesqueries in his office.

The lights are dim and tinted green, the sickly shade of gangrene. Dr. Emeris is studiously scrubbing the metal exam table. Minus the rock walls, this could be a modern clinic.

"Ah, a new patient?" he asks, turning and looking as I enter.

With perfect timing, Zero wakes up. A groan curls up from behind my head, and then she twitches into consciousness.

I squeeze my arm harder over her legs and refrain from saying anything idiotic. "Nope, only here for a few supplies. She's going right back to her cell," I say, raising my voice and hoping somehow Zero understands she should be quiet.

I have no such luck.

"What the...what the fuck..." she mutters.

"Are you sure?" Dr. Emeris says, his expression too eager. "She appears to have some wounds. I would be glad to—"

"Nope, thanks, I'm good. Where's your morphine?" I grab up some wooden tongue depressors, and more gauze and tape. A tube of antibacterial salve finishes the easy stuff.

"Hey...hey. Let go of me, you dick." Tiny fists hit my back, but only once because she lets loose a short scream. She must've forgotten the broken fingers.

"It's right there on the counter. May I ask—"

"Thanks, I got it." I spot another medicine bottle and the name leaps out at me. *Rohypnol.* Perfect. I snag it along with the glass bottle of morphine and a syringe.

Striding out before he can ask any more questions, I ignore Zero's repeated protests for me to put her down.

People who look like they know what they're doing can get away with a lot, and the stories I've spread of people who try to stop me were quite colorful. Didn't have to exaggerate them too much, either.

No one I pass gives me a second look, even with Zero thrashing and growling behind me. She spits curses and invectives, which I hope do something to help her mood. She can call me whatever she wants and it won't offend me.

Her cell is straight ahead. The other prisoners make noises to protest her yelling, no doubt upset their relaxing stay is being disturbed. I juggle my supplies and her until I manage to get the door open and step inside. I've got to make this quick so I can go back and placate Costecu. Dumping her onto the mattress, I push her back when she tries to get back up. "Sit down, Zero."

I let her go to open the pill bottle filled with the tranquilizers, keeping an eye on her. Her vision must not have caught up quite yet, because she's not looking directly at me. "Take this."

"Fuck you," she replies, jaw working after the words leave her. I can not only smell her sweat, I can see it, too, a sheen across her face. She's in a lot of pain.

"I think we've gone over this," I say, not having the time to debate or play with her. Instead, I grab under her chin and shove the pill into her mouth before she can react. It takes a second to get ahold of her nose, and she tries to push up again, but it's trivial for me to shove her back onto the mattress. "Swallow the pill."

She glares. I hold onto her nose and mouth. She swallows, but not until after I worry about how long it's taking. Then I remember she's a selkie and can probably hold her breath for a long time.

"There you go. Just relax." I let go of her nose, but not her chin, keeping her in place. It shouldn't take long. Human medicines can have strange effects on those with higher metabolisms or different biology. After what seems forever, but must only be a few minutes, her eyelids flutter, her lashes brushing cheekbones. She's still glaring as hard as she can, stiff on the bed, but the medicine-induced sleep is winning out.

I wait a couple minutes after her eyes close, and then tap her on the cheek.

"Zero?" I tap her a bit harder, then poke her shoulder. Her mouth drops open and she snores.

Working fast now, taking advantage of the early stage of the knock-out drug, I take her hand and pull on each broken finger. They straighten with a snap and crunch, the bones resetting back to their normal positions. She jerks a little, but doesn't otherwise react. I let out the breath I was holding, and using the gauze I splint the tongue depressors to her middle finger. It'll have to do.

I replace the gauze on her toe, pulling off the bloody cloth. It sticks a little to her skin as I unwrap it, the blood clotted, but starts seeping out as I peel the bandage away. Spreading some antibacterial on it and then re-wrapping it with fresh gauze, it's the best I can do for now.

Last up, I stick the syringe in the bottle of morphine, draw a dose, and inject it into the vein in her arm.

While I'd like to leave the morphine and syringe with her for when she wakes up, I can't risk it. Someone might find it, or find it on her when she gets out, or she might try to use it for something other than dulling her pain. It's a variable I can't risk.

I should get up and leave before she wakes up, talk to Costecu and get him back where he needs to be, but I can't quite make myself stand up. In the dregs of light down here she looks peaceful. Sleep smooths out her features, un-wrinkling her angry forehead and relaxing the frown that's been permanently fixed to her lips since I broke out.

A thumb under her chin closes her mouth and stops her light snoring. My finger lingers there, despite myself, brushing against the soft skin behind her chin bone. Evil Drew would kiss her. Evil Drew would do a whole lot worse when faced with an attractive and roofied woman, but I'm not Evil Drew.

I kiss her anyway. A small one, a quick brush of my lips on hers. The feeling is unlike the one in the elevator. That one was strong and forceful, taken from her to show who was in charge. There's no need for asserting my dominance now. Instead, I do it to see what she feels like. Soft and a little warm is my answer.

Discomfort worms through my stomach, like I've done something far worse than anything I've ever done before, which is ridiculous. I've done worse things to her alone a mere hour ago. A simple kiss is harmless in the big scheme of things. It still feels wrong, yet I kiss her again.

Sucking in a breath, I push back, let go of her chin, and stand. Enough. I have things to do. I can't be spending all my time making out with an unconscious woman. It would be more fun if she was awake, anyway. I can imagine the angry sounds she'd make.

Shit, I've forgotten to give her a map to my cabin. In all the activity of breaking fingers and patching them up, it slipped my mind. Looking around, even though I won't find anything, I try to figure out where I'm going to get paper, much less a pencil. I could go all the way to my room then come back, but the odds of someone grabbing me on behalf of Costecu are high. I left him kind of abruptly, and the longer I'm not in front of him explaining myself, the angrier he's going to get. There's got to be something I can do without leaving.

Inspiration hits, and I grab the gauze and unroll a strip. Jabbing myself in the finger with the needle, I squeeze out some drops of blood, and use it to write on the cloth. I'll have to make this short and hope it's enough.

19 w 124 n

Once she gets on highway 124 heading north—*if* she gets on highway 124 heading north—I should have caught up with her. If not, well...at least she has a chance.

I flap the gauze in the air a few times to dry it off, then roll it up and stuff it in her hand. Can't miss that. With one more look back, I step out and shut the door on her, trapping her inside the hideous cell. I twist the lock before the door is shut all the way, and the bolt slides out. I twist the handle further. The metal resists, but something has to give, and it's not going to be me. With a cranky screech, the handle snaps and spins freely. I push the bolt back in, shut the door, and turn the knob so it looks like it's locked.

When she wakes up, she'll find the note, although whether she'll be able to read it in this light is unknown. She'll be sore, and still hurting, and a little groggy, but once it all passes I expect her to pace around. Anyone worth saving will try the door at some point, and when it opens the escape will begin. I need to have calmed Costecu and gotten Gil out of the way by then, or it's going to be a short escape. It might be anyway, but it's all I can give her without giving myself away.

I'm still not sure why I'm doing all this. I could play along and within a couple of weeks everything would fade. Except then I'd need a new source, which would be a huge hassle. Her angry eyes pop into my mind as I walk away, and the thought I'd miss them floats to the top like a helpful bit of driftwood. Maybe not everything would fade.

I shouldn't be thinking of this now. I need to focus on Costecu. Distractions are always dangerous. Georg meets me halfway there, hurrying along like a silent bat.

"Costecu wants—"

"I'm on my way there right now," I say, brushing past him, not slowing. There are times when having a reputation as being volatile and violent comes in handy, like when you don't want to talk to anyone.

"He's pretty—"

"Shut up," I suggest.

Georg shuts up, which annoys me a little more since I wanted an excuse to punch him. All these things happening out of my control make me cranky. I like to be in control. I push on the heavy doors to Costecu's stupid waiting room, taking some satisfaction in hearing the door guard's head clunk on the other side of the wood.

"Lindberg," Costecu says, turning around from pretending to browse his bookshelf, as if he wasn't waiting for me. His tone would be menacing if I were the type to get menaced. Behind me a soft groan wafts up from the doorway.

"Yes?" I force myself to stay calm. If I get agitated, he's going to get agitated right back, and he gets reckless and impatient when he's upset.

"Why did—" He stops and sniffs. "Are you bleeding?"

Forgot about that. "Yes. A splinter from the door."

"Hmm. Why did you let her anger you, and why did you knock her out?"

"Like I said, I guess I was tired. Still am. Sorry. No permanent harm, she'll be right as rain in the morning. Minus the fingers and toe, I guess. They'll be a good reminder."

"I'm not worried about her. I know we'll get her to talk," he says, with a certainty borne of confidence. He's right to be confident. Everyone talks.

"We will."

"I'm more—disturbed you lost your cool. She seems to affect you in some way." He pronounces his words slow and even, with an emphasis made to convey exactly how disturbed he is.

I'd hoped it wasn't so obvious. "I'm not sure what you mean."

"I'll give you another chance to redeem yourself tomorrow. Because I trust you." The way the word "trust" comes out of his mouth tells me how much he doesn't trust me. "I'm sure you won't fail in your duty again."

Costecu is notorious for turning on so-called allies at the drop of a hat. The only reason I've stayed on his good side for so long is I've always done what he asked without any questions. He thinks I'm too dumb to ask many questions, which is why he trusts me as much as he does. That might be in jeopardy if he thinks I'm not treating Zero like I would any other captive. He knew I was acting out of character, which turned on his alarms. Being paranoid is how he's survived for so long.

"I understand." If I didn't plan to be leading the womanhunt for Zero by this time tomorrow, I'd be more worried.

"Go. Tomorrow at noon we resume." He dismisses me with a wave of his hand, turning to scan through his bookshelves again.

"Yes, sir."

I head off to my room, kicking the still-unconscious body of the door guard on my way out. I need to nap for a bit and try to figure out how to keep Gil busy and occupied for a few hours.

Come on, Zero. Be the clever woman I know you are. Your future is in your hands now.

CHAPTER ELEVEN

Aideen

My throbbing toes wakes me, but what I remember first is Lindberg shoving a pill down my throat. Then the rest follows, toe, fingers, all of it. I try to sit up, but can't quite get my limbs to respond. Even in the pitch blackness it feels like everything is spinning, a haunted merry-go-round with Lindberg at the center.

Must be the after-effects of whatever he made me swallow. It doesn't make any sense why he'd drug me after he already tossed me back in my cell. Then I think of a horrifying reason why he might, and it's enough to send a shock down my spine, jerking me upright. Hands not quite under my control fumble, searching, even as the fingers ache. I heave a sigh of relief on finding my slacks still on. It seems unlikely he'd bother to put them back. I reach inside my underwear, testing for fluids or tenderness when my brain gets the signal through that I'm holding something.

I squish my fist a little tighter, feeling something soft, about the size of a pill bottle. Opening my hand up, I look down, but can't see anything. This damn lack of light is enough to drive me crazy. Prodding with the fingers of my other hand, it feels like cloth of some sort.

Before I can investigate further, my pinky and ring finger on my prodding hand catch my attention. I can tell they hurt a lot, but I won't dwell on the pain right now. The fingers seem to be stuck together. Setting down the mystery item in my lap, I use my uninjured hand to explore. As more parts of my brain unscramble, I identify smooth wood and rough cloth. Some sort of splint. I can't bend any of my fingers, and it's definitely cloth around popsicle sticks or something. Did Lindberg do this? Why?

The slow throb of my toe is my next investigation. I reach down, as careful as possible, and poke it. After the fire of agony fades, I'm able to discern it's also wrapped in cloth, probably gauze. It feels like it's about the size of a watermelon, and I'm not sure I'll ever be able to walk again in my entire life. Where are my shoes, anyway?

I move to get up and search, but then remember the mystery item I'd set down, and pat around to find it. If Lindberg gave it to me, I better hold onto it. When I can find some light, I'll take a look. Not for the first time lamenting the fact women's slacks don't have pockets, because fashion is a dick, I slide it under my bra strap.

Commencing the search for the shoe, I scoot around the cell on my butt. There's no way I'm standing yet, and crawling with one hand would hurt my knees even more. Feeling grumpy at how much this sucks, I get even grumpier when I can't find my other flat. Now not only will my toe be destroyed, I have no way to keep it clean. Images of rusty nails jabbing into my foot reel about my mind, heedless that a thin shoe wouldn't actually help. I don't need germs crawling into my wound.

Dragging my sorry carcass back to the damp, straw-filled mattress, I ponder the state of things. All these injuries and still locked away in utter darkness with a bucket I'm supposed to poop in.

"What's happened to my life?" I shout in frustration. The only answers I get are some louder groans from nearby. Unhelpful ingrates.

I can't get depressed or down. Every minute I'm not strapped to the chair is a minute I could be working on getting out of here. I need to escape, get home, and take a bath to wash this whole experience away. How, I'm not sure, but that means I haven't thought enough.

Trying to calm down by picturing standing in the rain, I go over my options. They boil down to giving up or fighting back. Neither one is appealing. Though I'm back in this putrid cell, and adrenaline isn't controlling everything I do. The thought of again attempting to goad Lindberg into killing me is frightening in the extreme. If I hadn't been there myself, I wouldn't have believed anyone who told me I did it. I hope whatever place I tapped into comes out again the next time, because I won't be able to do it myself.

Except, there won't be a next time, because I'm getting out of here. Right? Absolutely.

Maybe I can fashion some sort of makeshift moccasin for my bare foot. I shrug out of my blazer and work at the seams of the sleeve. While I tug at the stitches, which are quite strong, I think back over the questioning.

Lindberg, his large frame blocking my view all the time. The way he'd snapped my pinky with no effort, like he was flicking away a bug. The strange look he'd given me while he was pulling my toenail out, which he did as easy as breathing. The man is powerful, I'll give him that. If he'd been on the right side of the conflict, it would be over by now. I'd send him into battle with no doubt he'd drag back all our enemies, a bit flattened, but ready to talk.

I see why Costecu uses him. From the moment he'd slapped me to get me to wake up, he's always been in control. Of me, of everyone around him. Even when talking to Costecu, Lindberg radiated an aura of the one who was in charge, like he could have walked out of the conversation at any moment. So why he had snapped when I needled him? It wasn't even harsh, and I'm sure he's heard worse.

The stitches give way, and I don't have to worry about the mystery of Lindberg anymore. Now I have to puzzle out how to wrap my foot in a way that doesn't hurt and also won't fall off the second I stand up. It's a bit of a struggle, but I get it all secured, and stand to test it. Keeping most of my weight on my good foot, I hobble around like a ninety-year-old woman. All seems in good order, until I kick the bucket with my bad foot, scream, stumble, and lurch into the door.

Instead of the hollow thump I expect when hitting the hardwood, I get a different type of thump when the door swings open and I land on the stone outside my cell. The door bounces off its hinges and comes back to knock me in the head.

"Ow," I mutter, blinking to clear the pain in my head or my foot, either one would work. Realization dawns—I'm outside the cell, the door slowly swinging back to open. A few more blinks and I push up to my foot, using my good hand to pull up the wall.

"Oh, shit."

Someone's been careless. There's no way I'm this lucky.

It could be a setup, a way to make me attempt an escape. Then they'd grab me again, right as I'm about to get out, drag me back to my cell, and I'd be at their mercy. Except I'm already at their mercy. It might be a morale-breaking move. Lift my hopes up only to crush them back down when I'm captured again. Make me think escape is hopeless.

They won't crush me, though, not if I'm prepared mentally. If I expect to get captured, then when I do, it won't matter. What's the harm in trying? I'll get killed? Already headed there. Perhaps I can put up a fight and get my neck snapped or something when I'm not paying attention. As much a fight as I can manage, with one leg, one hand, and teeth.

Good sense tells me to gather up stuff and prepare for this escape, but what do I have? Nothing. No reason to bring the poop bucket. Hesitating, considering it as a weapon, I shake my head clear of those thoughts. I'm not that desperate.

Orienting myself by standing in front of the door to the cell after I shut it behind me, I try to remember the path Lindberg pulled me on to get here. I was conscious both times so I'm confident I can retrace them back to the elevator and freedom. A few seconds of thought and review, and I turn down the hall. Taking cautious steps, in case there are bumps, I also keep my good hand trailing down the wall. Cool stone transitions to wood as I pass by several more doors.

A diffuse light comes from my left, almost unnoticeable except it's the only thing to pierce the darkness. I feel like a desert wanderer who's spotted an oasis in the distance, and relief floods through me at the simple grey stone it reveals—the passage to the left I need to take. I stop before passing through, giving my eyes time to adjust as much as they can to the smidgen of light.

I should also focus on listening, but all I hear is those moans from everyone else. I'll almost miss them. Their noise has turned into some sort of organic wave machine.

Peeking around the corner, I see nothing but more stone walls. As I round the corner and advance at a slow limp, the sounds fade behind me. This place is quiet enough to be creepy, and I can't think of a reason why there's no one about. There must be a fair amount of creatures living here, so the dank silence is off-putting.

Another thick wooden door blocks my path forward, and I stop next to it to listen. The wood is smooth under my ear, like it's been rubbed down by countless years of hands and shoulders pushing on it. No sounds waft through.

Grasping the knob and turning as slow as I'm able, I pull the door open a crack and peek through. It's a bit lighter on the other side, and I'm able to discern no other sign of life. Slipping through, closing the door behind me, I keep moving.

If I strain my hearing to the limit, I can pick up voices from somewhere, but the direction is uncertain and vague. All sorts of side passages are appearing, but I don't remember going anywhere but straight for this part. The next turn was after stairs, which appear in front of me with amazing timing.

At the top, I have a moment of confusion between left or right. One way is out, the other is torture, but which was it?

Daring to squeeze my eyes shut, I try to remember the march Lindberg took me on when I came in. After the audience chamber with Costecu, we went back into the main hall, turned down a hallway, steps—then he turned right, I think. So I need to go left.

The subtle fact this journey is also taking me closer to Costecu before I can get out is not lost on me. As long as I avoid going through any large doors, I should be okay. Unless he smells or hears me. I'm not sure how far away he can hear hearts beating, but the agency has noted it can be quite a distance with older vampires.

My heart pounds harder in anxiety, and I stop to lean against the cold stone to gather myself until I'm no longer scared someone's going to come upon me. If it happens, it happens.

Limping along on one foot is harder than I would've thought. Since I can see now, I take the opportunity to check the makeshift bandage over my damaged foot, then remember the cloth I found and tucked away. Pulling it out of its safe spot, I see it's a bit of rolled gauze. I unroll it. Smudged on it in what looks like dried blood is a cryptic series of letters and numbers. A code of some sort, maybe, but I'm not sure what to do with it. I'll keep it in mind, but right now it's useless to me.

I need to move again before I risk discovery. My luck has got to wear out soon. Maybe everyone is asleep? If it's daytime, that might be the case, but surely they have some people awake for security reasons. Costecu might be arrogant, but he's not sloppy, and neither is Lindberg.

As I progress through this dungeon, the tightness in my chest gets worse by the second. Any moment someone could swoop down on me haul me back to that horrible cell. I keep telling myself it doesn't matter. I'm already locked up, captive, captured, but having this slice of freedom is not something I want to lose. I miss my bath and everything it stands for.

I turn a corner, and without any warning, I'm in the main hall. Biting my lip to stop the gasp, I smoosh back against the stone wall, looking around in a panic for any of the opposition. To my right are the large doors I'd been escorted through before. Those voices I heard are louder now, and coming from behind it. Someone is shouting.

Taking the steps out into the empty hall is the hardest thing I've done, fearing every second to hear a shout of discovery, but I need to take advantage of this seeming distraction and get out while I can. Any hesitation could bring disaster.

As quick as my damaged foot allows, I limp off to the left, away from the door. My back prickles with tension, even as I push the button of the elevator, the only modern conceit in this whole place. I tense, waiting for the ding, which will shatter everything, but as the tension gets too high to stand, I remember it doesn't ding and a huge breath expels this particular worry.

The doors slide open before I have time to think about someone being in the elevator, and I stagger inside, shielding my eyes. I resist the urge to sag against the wall, because I'm not out yet. I have to face what I've been avoiding this whole time: the dragon.

This is where my short-lived escape ends, I'm sure of it. He'll snatch me up, and by the sound of the conversation on my way in, eat me on the spot. I hope he chokes on the popsicle sticks. No one will be able to say I gave up.

Like the crack of doom, the doors open at the speed of molasses, and the orange light inside the elevator spills out onto the cracked linoleum tile floor. I hold the doors back from closing, waiting for a roar or a shuffle. Waiting for a hulk to round the corner and spot me. Nothing happens.

A careful step out, then another, and I stand in the old entry, waiting again. The soft thunk of the metal doors bumping together behind me almost causes me to jump out of my skin. I wait for the horrible creature to appear around the wall and bite me in half, but there's no movement.

Slow and careful, and as quiet as I can manage, I creep forward. He could be toying with me, waiting for me to stick my head around the corner before he bites it off. At least it'll be quick. I won't even have time to recognize my end before it's upon me. The thought gives me a burst of courage, and I take the last steps forward.

A bold step around the corner, and I draw up to my full height to meet my demise with dignity. My eyes take a moment to penetrate the gloom in the nook. The whole room is empty. No one is here.

I blink a couple of times in case my vision has been compromised by the darkness or the drugs. Still nothing.

"Okay," I mumble out loud, the sound jolting myself out of disbelief and into the dull warmth of stupefied acceptance.

The door to the outside doesn't have a keypad, and so I don't need the bloody code on the gauze. I turn the knob and step outside.

The cool night air caresses my skin, and I could laugh at how ridiculous this whole thing has been, but my practical brain reminds me I'm not out yet. They could find out my cell is empty at any moment, and it won't be hard to track me by scent alone.

Determination pushes me down the block, toward where the stolen truck is. With any luck it's still there, and in thirty minutes I'll be safe back at headquarters.

I'm free.

CHAPTER TWELVE

Druain

Minus the couple restless hours before, it's been about thirty-six hours since I woke up in the concrete cell in Zero's base. My muscles ache and my eyes itch. I should try to take another nap and stay refreshed, but I'm too worried about Zero. I've given her the means to get out by leaving her door open, but I don't feel comfortable leaving it at that. She's proven to be clever, but going up against a whole horde of people won't make for good odds.

Sitting on the edge of my bed, I roll my shoulders. First thing to take care of is Gil. I need to get him a snack so he'll let me take a couple hours at the front door. If I do it too early, though, he'll come back before she's even awake. Is she going to shrug off the effects quickly, or be groggy for a while?

Once she gets out, how am I going to keep her safe? I'll have to be out of my room, but I can't be seen. Even the most tenuous connection could be enough for Costecu. He's already suspicious, and if he finds any excuse to connect me to the escape, I'm toast.

Which brings up another issue. If I'm supposed to be watching the door when she gets out, then he's going to know it was me. Shit. I need someone else to pin the blame on.

Georg would be perfect. The little weasel has been an annoyance for too long, always at my heels, trying to take my job. He even looks suspicious half the time, with his beady eyes and long, thin nose. I wouldn't be heartbroken if something happened to him.

The rest of the details fall into place without much effort. I spend some time exercising to stay awake and get my blood flowing. A couple hundred crunches to warm up, followed by as many push-ups as I can, arms burning until they won't work anymore. After thirty minutes I can't stand being cooped up in my room, so I take a quick shower to smell like soap instead of sweat, which could give my worries away, and then head toward the detainment area.

People are always surprised when they find out how light I am on my feet, but often are not surprised for long. I stand outside Zero's door after sneaking up to it, listening. Some rustling and muted grumblings come from inside, so she must be awake. A small hint of her scent lingers in the air seeping out from under the door. She could also use a shower.

Making my way back out of the area, I head toward Georg's room. He should be asleep. He shoots upright in an instant, in that creepy way vampires go from sleeping to awake, but his brain has a few seconds to catch up to his body. I can use those moments of confusion to my advantage.

"I need you to take the prisoner in cell five to Gil." Cell five holds a basilisk. I won't feel too bad about her disappearing either. Turned a whole family, including a nine-month-old baby, into stone just so she could have some lawn decorations. The only reason we went after her is because Costecu thought he could use her as a weapon, but she didn't want to help. Stubborn as a rock, she hasn't budged.

"Why?"

"Because I fucking said so, that's why," I say, stepping forward into his personal bubble. "I'll watch the door while Gil eats his snack."

Georg doesn't move, blinking at half the speed of a normal person.

"Go," I shout, punching him in the shoulder. "Are you trying to piss me off?"

With a grumble and a look backward, he departs. Good old stupid minions. Bye, Georg, and basilisk, and Gil might be in for a bit of trouble, too. I doubt Costecu will do anything serious to him, though. Vampires are a dime a dozen, but you don't ever run into dragons.

Needing to kill a few more minutes, I mentally run through the route Zero will take. The problem is, no matter which way she goes, she'll end up in the main hall. I need some excuse to clear it out. People are going to be waking up soon, if they haven't already, and there's a good chance someone will be there. It's the central hub to the web of corridors snaking through the entire complex.

I could tip someone off she's missing, which would mean Costecu would get a bunch of people into his room to yell, but that'd be cutting it close. We'd be in the room when she's sneaking by, and someone's going to be late, and someone's going to spot her.

Georg will be with the basilisk now.

Treading carefully, I head toward her cell, and when two pairs of footsteps approach, I duck into a side room. There's something about dwarves and rough-hewn rock—we tend to blend right into it. Tuck into a dark corner and most people will think I'm another bit of stone.

Georg and the basilisk walk by, not sparing me a glance. Once they're safely past, I continue on to the detention block. Zero's rustling around in there, and then a clunk and a string of curses bursts forth. I jump out of the way in time to miss being bashed by the door as it flings open and she tumbles to the hard floor.

Retreating as fast as I can without making any noise, thankful she doesn't have night vision, I back around the corner and start my patrol. Looking in each corridor I pass, I lock any doors I can. The ones that can't be locked or don't have doors I survey to insure they're empty.

It's not too hard to keep in front of her. Hobbled by the injured toe and not knowing the place, she doesn't set a blistering pace. I have a close call when I bump into a hobgoblin going to breakfast, but knock him out easily enough. Getting his body out of sight and keeping still as she passes five feet in front of me is less easy. The urge is strong to step out and carry her as she limps past like the saddest creature ever. I'm glad I took her middle toe, and not the big one, because then she'd have zero chance of getting anywhere. Even still, her determination is admirable.

The entry hall is next, and all I can do is hope because I'm behind her and unable to screen the room. I poke my head around the corner and hold my breath as she opens the last door and slips out of my vision, small as a mouse.

After a moment's pause I follow, but don't dare open the door. No howling, shouting, yelling, or screeching bursts forth, which is a good sign. There are regular voices and since they don't raise, they must be in with Costecu. I wait a couple more minutes, listening for any other clues of what's beyond, but there's nothing but silence. Cracking the door open, the soft swoosh of the elevator doors hits my ears. I let myself take a breath. As long as Gil is safely away, she should be good.

Now to figure out how to delay the discovery of the empty cell as long as possible.

"Lindberg."

The voice startles me, but I don't show it, turning to find Georg standing two feet from me. "What?"

"I thought you were going to watch the exit while Gil was away."

"I got caught up. I'm going there now. You're keeping me from going," I add with my best annoyed brow furrow.

"You've got a problem, then, because that bitch you brought in is gone."

Fucking shit. Just my luck this twerp would check after his errand. I raise my voice. "What? Are you sure?"

"Yeah, I was there like thirty seconds ago. Her door is wide open, looks like someone broke the handle, and she's gone." He's smirking, and I can imagine the wheels turning in his head, trying to figure out a way to knock me down a peg in Costecu's eyes.

"We need to tell Costecu now," I say instead of all the things I want to say, reaching out to grab him by the collar.

"Shouldn't we go look?" He flops about at the end of my arm. As if he has a chance of getting away.

"Really? You want to wait and then after an hour tell him she got out an hour ago? You think he's going to like that?" I fling open the door to the entryway and drag him after me. This moves things along quicker than I like. The distraction I'm going to make now will have to be long enough for her to put a good distance between her and Costecu.

"Or we catch her and haul her back in front of him. She can't have gone far. I was down there getting the basilisk a few minutes ago."

"If you want to waste your time, go ahead. I'll take the credit for finding out she's gone myself." I release him, a bit of a risk, but I doubt he can resist the urge to suck up to Costecu with his discovery.

He can't, and after a few torturous seconds he heads to the large doors and knocks. "It's urgent," he says to the opening peephole.

"What is it?" someone grumbles from inside. I could help, but every second wasted counts.

"Let me in, you ass," Georg complains, pushing at the wood in frustration.

"What's it about?" the grumble asks again, unmoving.

"Come on, open the door, shithead." He doesn't want to give up his prize information, which would make the door open quicker. I can always count on people to be self-serving. Each second Zero can have to get away is precious. "One of the prisoners has escaped, and the boss is going to want to know about this one."

The hatch closes, voices get louder on the other side, and then one of the big doors open. Georg scuttles inside and I follow, slow and measured footsteps, remaining calm.

Costecu is sitting in his chair, looking agitated but not angry. He's waiting for the other shoe to drop before he gets nasty.

"Sir—"

I cut Georg off, stealing his glory and making sure I'm in charge of the conversation. "Moarte's escaped."

"I see. How long ago?"

"About fifteen minutes," I say over Georg's upset whining. He's standing in front of me, so I can't see his face, but I imagine it to be pathetic.

"Go find her, then. If she tries to get out, Gil will stop her." Costecu turns to go back to his business.

"Gil isn't at the door," I reply, once again cutting off anything Georg might say. I put a hand on his shoulder. Goodbye, buddy.

Costecu's head swivels around and he fixes me with a stare to melt fire. "Excuse me?"

"Gil isn't at the door." I grip Georg hard so he can't get away. "I caught this worm coming back from bribing Gil with your basilisk."

"What?" They both ask in unison. Costecu's voice is lower and quieter but filled with a lot more menace than Georg's disbelieving tone.

"Apparently he let Aideen out, snagged your basilisk, and then told Gil to go somewhere else to snack."

"No, I fucking—"

"I guess this is his way of trying to get me in trouble."

Georg opens his mouth and a slew of curses pour out then trail off as Costecu gets up and stalks over.

"Is this true?" he asks, fixing Georg with a stare like a snake.

"Of course not," comes the reply, but the inevitable fear of facing down an ancient vampire is taking its toll. Sweat beads on the back of his neck, and he swallows.

I'm as calm as a rock since I did nothing wrong and have nothing to fear. Obviously.

"Where is she now?"

"How—I don't know. Why would I know? Lindberg's lying to you."

Costecu looks up at me. I look back. I can't believe Georg would have the nerve to accuse me of something so treacherous. What a desperate ploy. There's no way he could have thought his craven plan to let Aideen out and frame me would work.

"Thank you, Druain," Costecu says after a handful of seconds.

"What? No." Georg struggles, but Costecu takes him by the arm as I let go. We all know what the calm tone of voice portends. I step back while Georg keeps trying to get away, shouting and pleading.

"Thank you for your service," Costecu says, ever the fake gentleman.

I don't look away.

In a flash, his mouth gapes open, and I have a moment to catch a glimpse of the elongated fangs before he bites into Georg's throat. A scream erupts from the soon-to-be corpse, and everyone in the room backs up a step. They don't want to get splashed.

Crunching and nasty squishing sounds pierce through the screams. Costecu chews through the flesh in seconds, reducing the distracting wail to gurgles as the vocal cords are shredded. Georg flaps around like a fish on a hook as jets of his lifeblood flee his body.

Costecu bites again, deeper, pulling Georg's head back with thin fingers. I can see the edges of the gaping wound, although the blood pumping out is covering a lot of the details. Bright red pours down to puddle at their feet. Louder crunching echoes around the room like small firecrackers, and Georg stops moving, going limp as his spinal cord is severed.

With a final bite, Costecu detaches his teeth from the bone, then grabs hair and twists, snapping the head off the body. His face is bright red, dripping and wet. He closes his eyes and takes a deep breath as the body slumps to the floor in a puddle of blood. Slow spurts of the crimson fade as the heart gives out.

"Delicious," Costecu mutters, licking his lips, leaving a ring of clean skin surrounded by flecks of skin and Georg's blood. He takes a couple steps back and slumps into his chair. After a feeding he gets drowsy, filled and satisfied. The head dangles from Costecu's grip, turning back and forth, eyes wide and staring into the void.

"I'll get this cleaned up, and personally oversee the search to get Moarte returned. She can't have gone far." Glancing back at Georg's empty eyes, I allow myself a smile before addressing his lifeless remains. "Nice try, asshole."

"Yes, you do that, Lindberg. Good job. Keep me apprised." Costecu's fingers relax, and the head thumps to the floor, topples over, and doesn't move.

"Get this thing staked and burned," I command, turning to the nearest onlooker, yet another vampire I don't remember. "And then wash the floor. I want you to do it personally, understand? I'll be back to check."

He nods, his gaze flicking around the carnage before skittering off.

"You and you, come with me." I point to two other random minions—it doesn't matter who they are—and march out of the room.

Instead of taking the elevator to go find her, because she's probably only a few blocks away, I head to the mess hall. Most people hang out there when they aren't out and about, so it will be the best place to recruit. If only we had some way to instantaneously communicate with everyone in the organization, some form of "electronic mail," getting this all sorted out would be easy. For once, I'm glad Costecu doesn't like email. Now I can waste a good hour or two getting stuff together.

I'm all in with getting Zero out of here. If I could have taken out Costecu by myself, I would have long ago. The first time I was face to face with him in his room alone, I almost attacked him. It would have been foolish. Strong as I am, I can't take on a vampire of his age by myself. I need Zero, her resources, and her people to take him out. Once he's detained I'll figure out how to make him pay for everything he's done to me.

The people already in the canteen look up, conversation dropping away as I start talking.

"You," I say, stabbing a finger into the chest of one of my new lieutenants. Her name is Avestra, maybe. "Gather up some people. I need a banshee, wights, get that werewolf, what's his name, Lukas, any of your vamp buddies, and find me Gil. Bring them here. Go."

She runs off, and I turn to another one, a gnoll with a broken nose and hunched shoulders. "We're going to need transportation. Get me SUVs. Anyone you think can help you, get them, too. I want ten vehicles here fueled up in two hours."

I watch with satisfaction as he canters away to do my bidding. "Anyone here want to help find a fugitive?"

Hands go up.

Dropping into a chair, I lean back and smile. I'm now in charge of finding the woman I let out. There's one more bloodsucker out of my hair, and Costecu thinks I'm on his side.

This day turned out okay after all.

CHAPTER THIRTEEN

Aideen

The truck is no longer parked where Lindberg left it. Ten minutes of stumbling along pockmarked sidewalks with a swollen and bound foot and I have nothing to show for it. Nothing except several pairs of hostile eyes turning on me from across the street.

The cover of night makes people bolder, but even if it was the middle of the day, I'm one woman alone in the middle of a place with no other people but the thugs, who are staring at me. They approach like sharks.

"Well, hey there," one says as I'm encircled. "You look familiar."

All five of them leer at me. I should be afraid, I suppose, but they're all humans, not one of them are taller than me, I'm tired, and my foot is on fire. I don't have time for shit like this. The temptation to let go and chew someone's arm or leg off is strong, but not an acceptable action. If I reveal I'm not human and leverage my abilities over them, I'm no better than Costecu. I still have my brain.

"Yeah, I was here earlier with my husband." Not sure why I picked husband out of all the possibilities in the universe. I should've said boss.

"Oh, yeah." Five pairs of eyes look around for any hint of my pretend husband. "Where is he?"

"He's not with me." No use in trying to lie about it. I can still use their fear to my advantage.

"Well, that's too bad." Their slow grins come back. "He coming back soon?"

"Nope. You could do whatever you want to me right now. Rob me, kill me, rape me, and he wouldn't find out until tomorrow morning."

One who must be smarter looks worried, perhaps sensing this conversation is not going in a way favoring them. The rest smirk harder.

"You ought to be more worried, girl," the leader says, reaching into his pocket.

I ignore his warning, and stare straight into his eyes. "But then when tomorrow morning rolls around, and I'm not in his bed, he's going to come looking. He's going to know I came this way. He's going to remember you."

"So? We aren't going to be here tomorrow morning," he sneers, no backing down, but a couple others are showing doubt.

"That's smart. You know what my husband does? You wondered at all why we're even out here in the middle of nowhere?"

"No." He looks baffled, as if I asked him if his ears grew on his knees.

"He's an assassin." It's not too far from the truth. "Not like those you see in movies. He kills without thinking. He'll find you, every one of you, and he won't hesitate to take you out."

A couple mumbles emanate from a couple of mouths. I better push while I've got them worried.

"I can take care of myself, too. I'll definitely take out one of you before I get overwhelmed. Maybe two. Which one of you is feeling lucky?" I stare each of them down, one by one, and they all look away except the leader.

"Yeah, maybe, but you'll still be dead," he says.

"I've had a good life." I shrug. "I'll die happy knowing my husband will take great pleasure ending your miserable lives."

One backs up, then turns to fade away to their little camp under the highway. One by one the rest trickle away, until the leader turns with a scowl and stomps away in disgust. Cowards are only held together by strength, which is why Costecu is doomed to failure once Lindberg is out of the picture.

I better make a convincing exit, or they might change their mind. I keep going the way I was, which should go back to the highway. I still need a car, though. No one's going to pick up a hitchhiker in the middle of the city.

When I've put some distance between me and the thugs, I peek around, and seeing no one, duck into an alcove of another factory. My foot is hurting more than ever, the toe pulsing like the heart of a star.

A street light flickers across the way, only making the night seem darker. The buzz as it flips between semi-on and sort-of-off fills the space between the silence of an area with not enough people. There aren't going to be any cars here. None that run, anyway. Anything left behind will be abandoned and stripped for parts. Faced with a whole night of walking on this ruined toe, exhaustion seeps in.

Sinking down to the concrete sidewalk, I curl up around my knees. I haven't slept more than four hours in a long time, but this feels even worse. However much sleep I got back in the cell has been used up, and then some. As I go to wrap my hands around my knees, I'm reminded my fingers are broken. The sharp pain displaces the dull throb of my toe for a couple of seconds, and it's a relief to feel something different.

I almost succumb to the small part of my brain that wants to collapse into a puddle of tears and give up. It's nefarious, insistent, and persuasive. Instead, I bite my tongue, clench my good fist, and push back to my feet. I won't get anywhere if I give up. Going down without a fight would be worse than dying.

Although I doubt it's a good long-term idea, I flex my fingers as much as I can, using the pain to distract me from my toe. With my luck I'll end up with crooked fingers, but at least I'll have days to look back on this and feel rueful. If I lay down on the sidewalk and don't get up, I won't have the chance to worry about crooked fingers.

As I'm thinking about everything but where I'm going, it's a pleasant surprise to find myself on the highway onramp. I don't want to take the extra time it would take to follow it, but I *really* don't want to stay down below, in areas where people and creatures can hide in shadows.

The lights up here all work, and although cars flash past, bullets from an invisible gun, and I'm alone. I focus on the steps, one after another. Good foot in front of bad. The good foot is hurting now from walking and standing in this damn shoe that's only made for office environments. When all this is over I'm going to buy a new pair of sneakers and wear them all the time. Screw fashion and screw convention. I'm also not going to go into a room with a prisoner unaccompanied, but there's no need to dwell on mistakes.

In about three hours I'll be back at headquarters. I look up to find the moon, halfway to being half, a fat crescent of dirty white. No stars show through the haze of a city at night. Can I tell the time by the position of the moon? It's not like the sun, is it? I'm not sure. The only thing I'm positive of is it's night, and I'm tired, and I want to go home and take a bath.

I should be worried about someone coming after me. Lindberg and company racing up the highway and snatching me back, but I'm too tired. At this point I can't worry about anything more than five seconds ahead of me.

I scratch my shoulder, and have a moment of panic at a lump, mind jumping to cancer of all things before I realize it's the scrap of cloth with the numbers on it. Who gave it to me? The only answer I could think of was Lindberg.

There wasn't the opportunity for anyone else to do it. He choked me out, I woke up being carried by him to my cell and I didn't have it then. He drugged me, and I guess fixed my fingers and toes, and must have handed me the note, unless some doctor repaired me and gave me the note. I have no idea.

Thinking is distracting me, though, so I keep at it. If Lindberg gave it to me, what would be the purpose? Passing a note implies he thinks I'll get out. Is it possible he engineered my escape? The dragon, whatever his name was, wasn't at the door, which seemed like a stroke of luck. The odds my door would be open and the way out of the underground facility would be unguarded feels too monumental to be coincidence.

The mystery of what the note's supposed to be and who I'm supposed to give it to holds my attention for a while. I wander along those paths before circling back to what it means that Lindberg possibly gave it to me.

He could be the mole.

Lights sweep in front of me and the sound of an engine slows behind me. They've got me. I wonder if they're going to kill me or not. I keep walking.

"Miss?"

The voice doesn't sound angry, it sounds worried. I turn and am blinded by the headlights, colors dancing across my protesting vision.

"Miss, are you okay?"

It's a male voice who doesn't seem like anything but a concerned person. I can't see them, only a blob standing behind his door. I don't want to step forward and seem threatening, so I stay put. I work my brain up to having a conversation. "Yes, I'm fine."

"Are you sure? Walking along a highway at midnight? Have you been robbed?"

"No, but I could use a ride."

There's a pause. I imagine he must be surveying my poorly bandaged foot, a sleeve ripped from my blazer, my hair is a tangled mess, who knows what sort of dirt and blood is smeared around. He probably thinks I'm a junkie.

"Where to? A hospital?"

I let out the breath I'd been holding. He might be some crazy lunatic playing an innocent who kidnaps women who won't be missed. I'll take that chance. I walk forward, slow, toward the passenger side of his car. "No. Take me to the Connor Tower, please. Thank you so much."

The lock clicks on my side, I open the door, and slip into the seat. My vision adjusts. He's an older man, wrinkles around his eyes, which are concerned. His mouth is turned into a line conveying caution. "Connor Tower? You sure, miss? Looks like you could use a doctor."

"I'll be fine. I can, um...I know someone there. Thank you, again."

"No problem."

The car eases into gear, moving back onto the highway. The lights overhead strobe through the windows. I try not to, but the soft seat lulls me to sleep within a minute.

I wake up to a soft shaking of my shoulder. "Miss? We're here."

I'm still alive and not kidnapped again, so that's a plus.

"Thanks. Um, I don't have any money or anything." I put my hand on the handle in case I need to make a quick break for it, but if I was going to be in trouble it would have happened already.

"Don't worry about it. Remember to pay it forward when you can."

I haven't heard anyone say that phrase before. "Okay. Have a good night." I open the door and step out, my foot ramping up to throbbing in no time. The rest was nice, but now I almost feel worse. I'd gotten used to the fifteen minutes not on my feet, and now I have to get them used to walking again.

Stumbling up the wide marble steps, the lobby visible through the glass is lit by the dim orange lights. There will be at least one security guard, maybe a person or two. Enough people live here there's always some activity. I don't want to get stopped. I want to get into base, let everyone know I'm safe, do whatever reports I have to, and then go home. I should go to the ER, too. Maybe after the bath.

The car with the nice older man drives off, and I'm halfway up the stairs when I see some movement in the lobby. Someone is waving, looking right at me and waving. Not at me, but at someone behind them, beckoning the second person forward. The end of this adventure is near. I sigh in relief.

A muffled crack and then a shatter pierces the air like lightning. The window of the door in front of me blows out, sparkling in the night like the unseen stars in the sky. I slam to a halt. Another crack rings out, and I drop to the stairs even before I fully understand I'm being shot at.

The people in the lobby are shouting, more people are there now. They're pointing, a couple of them are running toward the door. They have guns, and they're out, and they're pointed at me.

There's no time to wonder what the hell is going on. I roll down the steps, keeping as low as possible. In my panic I forget my fingers again, jamming them against one of the edges of the stone steps. Shock propels me forward, scuttling off to the side along the bottom of the steps, hunched low, making my way toward the cover of the decorative marble planters.

"Don't let her get away," someone shouts. Amid the chaos of the moment, I recognize the shouter as Jackson. Why is he shouting, and why are they trying to capture and shoot me?

Another shot flings up a chip of marble above my head, making a sound too much like a hornet embedding itself in flesh. I crouch and run, my injured foot crying out as I abuse it by putting my weight on it. Reaching the edge of the planters, I pause a moment, but more cracks get me moving.

I dash across the gap as voices pursuing me are getting closer and closer. There's no chance of me outrunning anyone. I don't have any plan yet, so running is all I have. My feet pound the pavement as I make for the corner of the building, the hard concrete sending thuds up my shins through the thin coverings on my feet. What I need to do is get into shadows.

Though the breath is searing my lungs, the voices are gaining on me. Around the corner is brief safety, but no time to pause. With a growl I reach down and yank off my flat. My little toe is chafed and blistering from being squished. At this point I'd rather step on glass than feel the burn anymore. The shoe flies off into the distance as I fling it with all my might, and a moment of vindictive satisfaction boosts my mood.

Now I'm faced with the problem of hiding somewhere. This is downtown, and I'm at the base of one of the tallest buildings here. There aren't a lot of shadows. Running along the wall, because I have no other choice, I churn through every ridiculous scenario of escape I can summon. Grow wings and fly away. Turn invisible. Climb the building. I look up, wondering how far I'd get. About five feet is my guess.

Voices change from muffled to clear behind me. "She's limping, she can't get far."

Why am I running from my own people? This is insane. If they hadn't shot at me multiple times, I'd consider turning around and surrendering, but another bullet whizzes into the building next to my head, ending that line of thought once and for all.

I zag into the street between two parked cars. There's no point in sticking to the building, and I don't want to get caught in some pincer movement. My feet are numb, which is helpful since now I can ignore them. For some reason my nose decides to let me know how smelly I am. Sweat and fear, and a lingering scent of shit bucket plus rancid meat.

Across the street a line of young trees marks the edge of the sidewalk. They don't provide much cover, but it's still cover. My former colleagues are calling out to each other, coordinating, but the words are lost to the pounding in my ears and the hot air in my lungs.

The next corner comes up, and I zip around it as fast as I can, pushing the sounds behind me away. Don't think about how much closer they're getting. I see nothing in front of me to help, so after a short detour around the building to leave line of sight I shoot across the street again.

Metal tears into metal as another bullet goes wide. They're being so reckless. They shouldn't be chasing me in the open, even if it's at night, unless there is imminent danger. Last I checked, I'm not imminent danger, so why am I being treated as such?

Thoughts are scattered as a police car rolls into view. My hands shoot up in the air and I let out a shout. "Help. Hey."

The car doesn't slow right away, but when I dart out in front it does. I run up to the window, out of breath and I'm sure looking like a crazy person. The window rolls down.

"Are you okay ma'am?" The cop's middle-aged, a slight paunch, not the best I was hoping for. A young cop would be all over helping me. This guy has eyes that have seen everything and stopped caring.

"There's—there's—" I struggle to catch my breath. "Men. Chasing."

He looks over my shoulder. The night is silent. "Are you sure?"

"Yes. Yes. They probably…saw you and—" The metal of the car is cool, and I lean my forehead against it, sucking in what air I can get. My toe thumps again, coming back to the front of my problems.

"Mmmhmm," he replies, in a tone of voice that says he's not convinced. I bite my tongue so I don't say *stupid fucking cop, do your job*.

"Can you—take me—hospital…" I'm not sure where else to go.

He pauses, and I think he's about to say no, but then sighs and the back door clicks open. "Get in."

"Thank you. Thanks." I tumble into the back and slam the door behind me.

He says nothing as he drives off. For all I care, he's taking me to his station for some imagined offense, which would be okay at this point. I'm dozing off when his radio crackles to life, and judging by the code, it's a possible DUI a couple blocks away. He pulls off to the side.

"Sorry ma'am, I need you to get out of the car. I need to take care of this."

"But—"

"Ma'am, please get out of the car," he repeats, stepping out and pulling my door open.

"Please, can I—"

He grabs me by the shoulder and tugs me out. "Sorry, ma'am. Hospital is a few more blocks. Enjoy your night."

I'm left standing on the sidewalk, mouth open, not believing what happened as he roars off with his sirens going. I wish I'd gotten his badge number so I could report him. I laugh. What else can I do? I stand on the sidewalk for what seems like forever, brain turned to mush. The hospital is only a few more blocks. I can walk there. Five steps later I slide down the wall of whatever building this is.

Ducking my head between my arms and knees, I grip my shoulders. The bump of the cloth meets my fingers, and I reach and tug it out like a lifeline. Something to focus on.

19 w 124 n

Closing my eyes for a minute, taking a breath, I open them and study the cryptic message. If I can figure it out, everything will be okay. Right? I need to figure this out.

It'll be okay.

CHAPTER FOURTEEN

Aideen

Tucked against the corner of the building, the night streaming over me, I think about the message in my hand rather than everything that's been happening.

19 w 124 n

It's so short. Not a safe combination—I don't think any safes use letters. For a minute or two I consider it being coordinates, but north only goes to ninety, which is the north pole. It has to be west and north, but I can't think of any other words N or W would stand for.

I tip my head back to rest against the concrete of the building, staring at the sky, wondering if I even want to follow whatever instructions or message this is. It still could be an elaborate trap, but it seems unrealistic someone would set this whole thing up. There's no clear purpose for it.

The muted green street sign under the orange glow draws my eye, a little splash of color in the dim light. 24th and Pine. Both streets. How do they decide if it's a street or a road or a way or whatever else? East 24th Street. Pine Street.

I blink. East 24th Street. E 24th St. I look at the crumpled gauze. *19 w 124 n*. There's a 19th Street, but there isn't a 124th, and even if there was it would be east or west. I think 19th Street ends in some residential area. Maybe it's supposed to be a street and an apartment number, but there aren't any apartments there.

I push to my feet and limp back and forth a little to get my blood flowing, trying to inspire my brain. After only a few seconds of pacing, lightning strikes. Highway 19 runs right around the city, and a bit west along it State Highway 124 intersects it, going roughly north and south.

Now I have to decide if I should go there to find whatever I'm supposed to find, or go to the hospital to get fixed up. My apartment is out of the question. They're either there or about to be there. They might go to the hospital too. Steinitz Medical Center is close by, and it wouldn't be too crazy to send a couple people to cover it. I would. I'd cover their house, hospitals, any family they have, police stations.

Might as well go see what's at this mysterious location. It's an unknown, but at this point it's better than nothing. There's no way in hell I'm walking thirty miles out of the city, though. I need a car.

It wouldn't be as easy as Lindberg made it look with the old junker. I have no idea what wires to touch together, and I suspect it only works on older cars. There are only a couple of vehicles parked along the street, and they're modern. If it comes down to it, I'm not even sure if I could break the glass.

A car pulls to a stop at the light behind me and an idea forms. Before I can enact my plan, I need to leave a clue. Whoever gave the note to me—I'll pretend it's Lindberg—is going to need to know I'm going where they're sending me. I whip off my blazer, roll it up tight, and stuff the message inside before dropping it next to a parking meter. It's the best I can think of in the five-second window I've got.

"Help, help," I shout, running out into the street, channeling all my inner desperation and helpless woman vibes. For the first time I'm grateful I look as awful as I do. No sign of acknowledgement from the driver, and I can't see through the windshield to determine if I'm scaring the occupant, so I move around to the driver's side.

"Please, I need help," I repeat, placing my hand on the glass, peering inside. A woman's scared face looks back at me. I'd feel less guilty if it was a man, but there's nothing I can do about it. "Please."

My tangled hair, bandaged fingers on the glass, and limping gait must be enough to convince her I'm for real. Her window rolls down. I let out the breath I'd been holding.

"Do you need a ride?"

"Yes, but no. Sorry. I need your car." I cringe in apology and then reach to grab the door handle on her side and pop it open.

"What?"

Humans tend to process shock at a slower pace, preferring to think there's some sort of mistake rather than accept something bad is happening to them.

"Your car. I need it. I know you don't have any reason to believe me, but I'll make sure you're compensated when I can." She's not wearing a seatbelt, so I tug her out onto the street. The car starts rolling, of course since her foot came off the brake. The door almost clips my legs out from under me, but I dip in and push the brake with my injured foot, gritting my teeth with the pain. Scooting over and switching feet helps, and the door swings shut behind me, leaving the stunned woman standing in the middle of the road.

"If I had any money now, I'd give it to you," I call out. "The hospital is a couple blocks north, go there. I'd ask you to wait to call the cops for a few hours, but that's probably too much to hope for. Sorry." I accelerate, turn left at the next light, and head toward the highway.

After about five minutes all the adrenaline from stealing a car wears off. I'm doing all sorts of new things these days, and none of them are from my bucket list. I want to sleep for a million years.

In an effort to stay awake, because I feel sleep creeping up behind my eyes like a cheetah stalking a gazelle, I roll down the window and stick my arm outside. The air flowing against my skin helps a little. Fall is sneaking up, turning the nights chilly and the days dimmer. Goosebumps form across my skin in the night, but it's still not enough.

Sneaking quick looks at the interior of the car, I find the window controls on my arm console, and roll them all down. To add a little extra insurance, I turn the radio on and find some '80s heavy metal music. The horrible sound of it grates over my ears as the air batters my face. Much better.

What I'm going to do when I get to the highway intersection is beyond me. I'm running on fumes and instinct. My brain is struggling to remember where I'm going. I chant the numbers in my mind, and then out loud, although I can't hear myself over the music.

"Nineteen west, one-twenty-four south. North. One-twenty-four north. Nineteen west, one-twenty-four north. Nineteen west, one-twenty-four north." It's only another twenty minutes of cold, dark, nerve-wracking driving.

I have no idea of my plan when I arrive. I guess I'll park the car somewhere, hide, and wait to see what happens. All while not falling asleep. I scan the dashboard looking to see if there's seat heating before realizing that would be a horrible idea. I slap myself, and the pain in my cheek matches the pain in my fingers, keeping me awake for another fifteen seconds.

I change radio stations to mindless pop and pretend I can sing along. The words don't matter, but the yelling disguised as singing does. Soon enough I'm full-on yelling, not even pretending to sing. Yelling at the world, at Lindberg, at flats, at vampires, at anything I want to yell at, because it's the middle of the night in the middle of nowhere and I can.

Someone passes me in the left lane. I resist hunching down in my seat. I'm not doing anything but driving along like a normal person, I'm not a banged up and half-delirious selkie going to a meeting with a psycho killer who's probably going to crush me between his hands.

After they pass I sing some more. The clock shows about five minutes left to my destination. That's when the nerves hit.

A wave of nausea sweeps over me, and I grip the steering wheel tighter even as my fingers complain with pain. Blinking fast, I let the pain center me again, and after a handful of long moments the anxiety subsides. It takes too much energy to maintain. I need all I've got to keep the car going straight. I'll let myself be anxious when I'm locked in a cell or bleeding out in the woods.

The green highway signs tell me highway 124 is in three miles. I push the gas pedal a bit harder, needing to be there and get it over with. With one mile to go I pull to the side of the highway and park. Taking a few minutes to clear my head, my eyes want to flutter closed so I jam the heel of my palm into them. Stay awake.

I turn the radio back to one of the presets and roll up the windows, leaving the key in the ignition. No reason to make it easy for anyone to steal or wreck the car. With any luck the authorities will find it before anyone else decides to try to take it.

The night air is chilly, and for the first time I regret the loss of my blazer. Buttoning the top two buttons on my shirt is more of a psychological help than anything else. The thin fabric provides almost no protection against the wind.

The thing about highways is they're not as smooth as you'd think. The shoulders are covered in gravel, and I regret impulsively discarding my flats. The scrap of cloth around my injured foot is in tatters. Good thing I can't feel those toes anymore. Gravel prickles the soles of my feet as I hobble off the side of the road. The rocks are bigger there, but there's also dirt and plants to soften the poking.

Walking the last three quarters of a mile or so to the highway intersection feels like it takes hours, but it must only be fifteen minutes. It looks like a couple of regular highways meeting. Two laned One-Twenty-Four arcs over the four lanes of Nineteen. The offramp goes up to meet it, and I imagine an onramp does the same thing on the other side.

I guess I'll wait to see what happens.

Surveying both sides for any remarkable looking places to hide, the only thing I see is scrub and trees, and grass. Any place would be as good as any other place. Deciding to be a little clever, I trek over to the other side of the highway and take up residence in some bushes on the side looking back toward the city. I'll be able to see any car coming, and anyone looking will most likely search the opposite side first, giving me time to get away if I need to.

The bushes aren't comfortable. A branch keeps poking me in the shoulder no matter which direction I push it or move it around. The ground is damp, and the slacks don't last long in keeping out the cold. In addition to sneakers, I'll be wearing jeans from here on out, and at least two shirts.

A cricket calls from a few inches away, loud and grating on my nerves. I wouldn't be surprised if it's some sort of vampire cricket, calling out my position. I thrash my good hand about in the brush, trying to dislodge it. It stops calling while I rustle and toss the branches around, but seconds after I cease my frustrated flailing it starts up again. Crickets must be the world's most advanced creatures. No matter how close they are you can never find them, and they never shut up. Another round of flailing leads nowhere.

"Shut up," I plead, having the sense to keep my voice low.

It doesn't listen, and in fact it chirps louder.

"You're such an ass."

To satisfy my rage, I turn and grab the branch poking me and twist at it until it breaks, a long strip of bark peeling off with it. I toss it down with a self-satisfied smirk. Take that, nature. I can beat you.

Occasionally, cars drive by underneath, either red or white lights searching out the road, splashes of color in the darkness. I wonder what it looks like to Lindberg, with his vision adapted to darkness. Would he be able to see into the cars? All I see is sharp black blobs speeding by, even the color sometimes hard to determine. Maybe that car is blue, or red, I can't tell.

My meager abilities versus Lindberg's is frustrating. Dwarves are strong, vampires are strong and fast, werewolves have a great sense of smell. Phoenixes are almost impossible to kill. Gnomes are fast and clever. Lots of species have amazing powers. So many can see or hear or smell well beyond what I can do. All I've got is my intelligence and a love of water, neither of which are special. Deciding to move to the middle of the country, surrounded by mountains, is something I wish I hadn't done. The reasons seemed good at the time, but now I want to be back in California, where the ocean is a short drive away.

My legs are cramping. I shift around, trying to get some blood flowing, fighting my aching muscles. If nothing happens in another fifteen minutes I'll get up and move to another spot for variety. Before I can get up, I see another set of lights coming from the city. I'll wait for the car to pass before I move.

Instead of driving by, though, the lights slow, and then merge off to the side of the highway. My heart speeds up. They've pulled up in front of the car I abandoned. It's too dark and too far away for me to see what's going on except for a bit of movement along the sides of the vehicles.

The cricket begins again and I jump and clamp a hand over my mouth. I hadn't even noticed it stopped. The headlights move forward, creeping along the highway and then up the offramp across the bridge from me. It's close enough now for me to be able to tell it's a dark SUV, nothing special or noteworthy about it.

It turns north up the local highway showing red taillights, and crawls a short distance, then stops. The lights blink out, sucking the darkness in and leaving me blinking to get as much night vision as I can. I hold my breath.

The driver door opens and I can see a shape in what moonlight there is. Tall and large, it has to be Lindberg. No one else is that size, except Abi the golem, and she can't drive.

The shape walks toward the bridge—long and slow steps, deliberate. The head turns, looking up and down the highway below, then down the road in my direction. It's Lindberg, without a doubt.

I'd recognize his beard even in the dark of night. I can't see his eyes, hooded under his brow, but I imagine they're like searchlights, scanning the ground. Looking for me.

He stops in the middle of the bridge, stands at the railing, and looks back the way he came. Then he turns, leans back against it and crosses his arms.

"Come on out, Zero," he shouts. "I know you're here somewhere."

I don't move. This is it, the moment when I need to decide if he's been playing me or helping me. My toe, my fingers, my legs, and my freezing body and tired eyes all vote for helping.

"I'm not going to hurt you. I can help."

I'm not sure I have a choice. I can't crouch in a bush the rest of my life.

Well, I could, but it would be a short life.

I chew my lip, take a breath, and struggle to my feet.

CHAPTER FIFTEEN

Druain

The organized chaos in the breakroom is more chaos than organization, but I do keep it moving forward. If things don't happen, Costecu will notice, so I have to keep at least a semblance of progress in case he comes to check.

Contradictory orders, "accidental" misinformation, and an atmosphere of tension created by a lot of shouting helps slow things down. I send the SUV squad out a second time, because they didn't get a van, which I one hundred percent didn't tell them to get but insist I did. After organizing everyone into five groups, I reorganize them a couple more times.

Gil shows up, storming into the room in the slow way large creatures have, bumping against the doorframe.

"What the fuck?" he rumbles, closing in on me, teeth showing a little.

"I didn't have anything to do with it," I reply, watching his talons click on the concrete. "It was all Georg. Costecu took him out already."

"He said you told him. Costecu took away my off-time for a month," he adds, look turning from anger to crestfallen. I see him like the dog next door who barks and looks fierce, but always backs away from the fence when you get close, until one day you find him sitting happily in the remains of your cat, blood all over his face. He's harmless until he's dangerous, and he's dangerous when he's upset.

"I didn't tell him, buddy." I stay seated. There's no need to make a scene. Everyone around us has stilled, watching. They're eager for a show. It's happened before, and Gil's undefeated so far.

His hands flex a little, the snick of scales against scales sliding around the room.

"Shouldn't you be at the door?" I ask, modulating my tone to be concerned. "I don't want you getting in more trouble."

He stares at me a moment longer, snout wavering a little and then dropping. "Yeah. I should. I wanted to come with you."

"Maybe next time. Was the basilisk tasty at least?"

"Yeah." He grins, executes a complicated turn, and trundles back out the door. The air in the room relaxes, but not without a tinge of disappointed murmurs. I hear he's seven-to-four odds in the pool, not that I'd ever participate in something so barbaric.

With him taken care of, I delay departure as long as I can. When it's bordering on the obvious I'm not taking this seriously, I make my way to the garage with the posse behind me.

Now, who do I like least? No more vampires for me tonight, and no one loud. A ghoul and a werewolf, although I might regret the wolf later. "Cashtor and Lukas, you're with me. Avestra, you take these two, you two together, and I want you with them, but no getting out of the SUV." I point and glare at the manticore. Like Gil, she's far too obvious to let out in public except in emergencies.

A few more divisions and some grumbling when I put a wight and an efreet together. That'll cause fireworks, maybe literally. The more they fight, the better.

"I'm going downtown," I tell them. There's a good chance she went back to her base, or maybe the hospital nearby. If I knew where she lived, I'd go there, too, but we've never figured out her address. I send the rest out to various other plausible but unlikely areas, telling the last team to spiral outward from the base.

Heaving up into the driver's seat of the newest looking SUV, I take off as soon as the others load in. The first thing to do is retrace my drive on the highway. It's the fastest by car, and while it might be a bit out of the way when traveling on foot, I'm not sure she'd brave some of the areas between here and downtown. I remember the thugs from earlier and cut to the left to make a stop. Maybe they're still there.

They are. I make a U-turn and pull up next to them and roll down the window. Before I can say anything, one of them notices me and leaps up.

"Oh shit. We didn't do nothing to her, man. I swear, she was like that before we saw her. I ain't getting killed for that." He turns and runs away.

Playing along, I raise my eyebrows at the rest of them. "Where'd she go?"

"I dunno. Like, that way," another says, gesturing to where I'd left our getaway truck. I'd be surprised if it or she is still there, but I need to go look.

I lean out of the window, draping my arm across the door. "Get the fuck out of here. I don't want to see you again."

They scatter like leaves out the back of a lawnmower. Lukas chuckles behind me, sounding like an eager rottweiler. "Stupid humans," he says. Cashtor remains silent like a proper ghoul.

I swing the SUV around again in the empty street and in less than a minute we're at where the truck was. Empty.

"What're we stopping for?" Lukas asks.

"Shut up and let me think." The offramp is a couple blocks away. The other way is darkness. There's no way she'd go there, I'm sure of it. I accelerate up the ramp onto the highway.

Cruising along at the minimum, I pull out my phone and tune in the police scanner. Ambient crackle and generic trouble come from the phone while I keep my eyes fixed on the shoulder of the highway. It's been long enough she shouldn't be up here anymore, at least not this close, but it doesn't hurt to be thorough.

The short cruise is uneventful, and nothing notable is happening in the way of crime by the time I exit the highway and head toward the Connor Tower. My companions are unimaginative enough to not ask any questions, they stare out the windows for any sign of trouble. A couple of blocks from my destination, I see flashing lights ahead, red and blue flickering against the night mist. I accelerate.

Five cop cars are parked in the road outside the front entrance of the tower, a couple up on the sidewalks. A few people mill around, drawn by the spectacle. A quick look shows no ambulances. Either they've already left or were never needed. I hope it's the latter.

The place where she works has a bunch of cops outside of it. There's no way it's a coincidence. Something happened, and I need to find out what.

Lukas growls low in his throat as we roll up even to the scene.

"You smell anything?" I ask, slowing but not stopping. I'm rubbernecking, no need to pay attention to me, Mr. Policeman.

"Humans. Non-humans. Fuck, I can't tell, the gunpowder is everywhere."

"Gunpowder? Shit. No blood?"

"No."

Cashtor doesn't react either. Neither one of these guys would miss a drop of blood. That's good. So who's shooting at who?

Of course. Understanding hits me like a boulder and I grip the steering wheel enough to whiten my knuckles. Our mole. Costecu must have contacted them in some way, told them Zero got out. They probably invented some reason to kill her so she couldn't reveal our location or other critical information.

Well, shit, then they're probably looking for her, too. Now I really have to find her first. If she tried to go here and was chased off, I need to figure out where the next place she'd go would be.

Driving another block and making a left to park behind the building, I reach into the console to pull out the shoe I'd taken off of her during interrogation.

"We're getting out, but no interactions," I say, glaring at each of the other two in turn. "Don't talk to anyone, don't look at anyone, don't bite anyone. Am I one hundred percent clear?"

They nod, not meeting my eyes.

"Good. Sniff." I hold out the shoe.

Lukas's nostrils flare. "Lemongrass and stinky feet. Why the fuck is it always shoes? Can't you get me like some panties or something? I don't have a fucking foot fetish."

"Feet..." Cashtor says, fingers reaching for her flat. I snatch it away and stuff in back into the console.

"You're sick," Lukas wrinkles his nose. "Stand like ten feet from me, dude. You're going to mess everything up with your stench."

I get out of the car and don't bother to hide my eyeroll. If I can get any help out of them before I get fed up it will be a miracle. They follow me, bickering, as we round the corner and try to stay out of sight under the building. The lights are still flashing on the next block at the base of the tower. At the corner of our street I hold out a hand to stop them. We'll need to check all four corners to see which way she went.

"Smell anything?"

Lukas sniffs, turns, sniffs, pushes Cashtor away and sniffs again. "Yeah. She was nearby. Or..." He pauses and then walks around the corner.

I follow, glancing to my left as we walk north along the opposite side from where we parked. The lights fade away behind us. No one's following.

He pulls up and I almost run into him.

"Found her other shoe."

I push Cashtor away before he can get his knobby fingers on it and pick up the grey flat. It's hers, all right, size eleven and a perfect match for the one in the SUV. For a brief flash I imagine she's Cinderella and I'm Prince Charming, looking for the foot to fit the shoe. I scoff and look at Lukas.

"Well? Where now?"

"Give me a fucking second, okay? This isn't magic." He paces up and down, then continues along the wall. "Oh, yeah. Strong here. She was right here. Going this way."

We round the next corner, and my eye catches on a small hole in the stonework of the building. I stick my pinky in it to feel a smashed nub of metal. "Bullet."

"No blood," Lukas confirms before running out into the middle of the street. "Whoa, okay, she stood here for a bit, but then it disappears."

I look up and down the four-lane street. It's empty, with a few cars parked in the spaces alongside. The pools of orange light break up the monotony of the dark night on unscathed blacktop. "She must have gotten in a car. Fuck. Can you follow it? Not a lot of traffic."

"I guess." He circles around the area.

"Cashtor, get the SUV and follow us." I throw him the keys. "Leave the shoe where I left it or I'll break your fingers," I warn.

He ambles off around to the other side of the building. Lukas walks west, taking us along the back of the Connor Tower. There's an entrance or two back here, but they aren't the public one with the nice lobby and steps. Only a sliding glass door as the entry. Lukas goes a couple more blocks and then stops in an intersection. Cashtor idles the SUV behind us.

"I don't know. There were a couple other cars here. They all mix in the middle. Some go straight, some turn right."

I find the signpost with the street names 24th and Pine. If we follow 24th it'll take us to the part of downtown with all the clubs and restaurants, which seems an unlikely direction. Up Pine, and then a couple streets over is Steinitz Hospital. While going to a hospital is something I should applaud, it means she hasn't figured out what I wrote. It also makes her easier to find, and the next place her people are going to check for her.

"She's going to the hospital." As I'm reaching for the handle to get behind the wheel and speed off, Lukas runs off up the road and then to the side.

"Get over here, mutt," I shout, not willing to wait for him to mark his territory. They're barely better than dogs half the time.

"No, no, dude, she was right here."

"What?" I let go of the door and run over. He's standing next to a little alcove, circling, but as soon as I get there he trails off up the sidewalk.

"Yeah, she was there, but then went this way."

I follow after him, but then I spot a bundle in the darkness and I push ahead. Dropped next to a parking meter is her blazer. I grab it in my fist, clutching it like I want to do to her. Stuffed in the middle of the rolled-up bundle is the scrap of gauze.

My mind spins, trying to decide what this means, torn between deciding if it was accidently left behind. Even if she dropped it on purpose, I don't have any idea if she understood what it refers to. I look at the scrawl again, and if I hadn't written it I wouldn't be able to guess, but I'm not as smart as her. I bet she can do those sudokus.

Lukas peers over my shoulder. "What's that? Smells like her. Whose blood is that?"

I shove the scrap into my pocket before he can get a good whiff. "Her blazer. Get in the SUV." I push him in front of me and climb in.

Sitting behind the wheel, I pause. The hospital is ahead. The highway is off to the left.

"What are we waiting for?" Lukas asks from the back seat.

I crank the wheel to the left and floor it. Sometimes it's better to act on instinct. If you sit and think about every decision, by the time you make one it'll be too late. Either she's at the hospital or on the way to the rendezvous point, and there's only one way to find out.

After it's clear we aren't going to the hospital, since I get on the highway and head west, Lukas speaks up again. "This isn't the way to the hospital, dude."

"We're not going to the hospital."

"Oh." He opens his mouth to ask another question, but then closes it again as he meets my glare in the rearview mirror.

Highway 19 going west meets Highway 124 going north about thirty minutes outside of the city. The ride is quiet for about fifteen of those minutes until I pull off onto the shoulder and turn off the engine, pocketing the keys.

"What's going on now?" Lukas asks. I don't answer him while I get out and come around to his side of the door. Cashtor is still staring out the front window, mind in whatever weird gutter ghouls seem to dwell in. Feet or ribs or kidneys, who knows.

I open the door and beckon Lukas out. "Come here, let me show you something."

"Okay."

I walk around to the back of the SUV and a moment later Lukas comes around the corner. I grab his shoulder, spin him around and lock him into a sleeper hold before he can react more than grabbing my arm, and by then it's too late.

I feel the pinch and scrape as his fingers shift to claws, and he attempts a howl, but six seconds is all it takes, as with any creature with a circulatory system. He goes limp, leaving a series of short claw marks on my forearm.

Moving with speed now, I stride to the passenger door and yank it open. Cashtor has smelled the small amount of blood on my arm and is turning to look, but I fist his stringy hair and pull him down into the open door. The sound of the door repeatedly slamming against his neck mixes with the guttural screeches burbling from his mouth. His hands push at the door but they can't stop me from my job. With a final slam his head comes off in my hand. Old blood oozes from the door, dark red and thick, the same dripping from the head like heavy raindrops. I toss it on the ground and stomp a few times until the skull splits like a rotten watermelon. After kicking it under the guardrail I open the door again.

Reaching across the now dead corpse, I unbuckle the seatbelt and pull the body out. With a heave it also flies over the rail, tumbling down the embankment into a copse of trees and rocks. My pants are splashed with thick ichor. Not the first time, and it won't be the last either.

Back around the rear of the SUV I put a foot on Lukas's chest, grab the top of his head and his chin, and twist until his neck snaps. Then, just to be sure, I pull out Zero's little pocketknife and cut between his ribs over his heart. My fingers are able to squeeze between the thick bones and I snap a few open. A little sawing and tugging and the heart comes out.

I wipe my red hands clean on his pants as best as I can before tossing everything over the side. If any of Costecu's crew comes this way they'll sniff them out quick enough, but I'm not going to let that happen.

Back in the SUV I start it up, turn the radio to a classical station, sounds like Mozart, and drive off. Fifteen minutes to the place where I hope she's waiting.

CHAPTER SIXTEEN

Druain

The slight wind blowing over the bridge cools my skin. I shouldn't be as nervous as I am standing against the railing and wondering if she's here. I'll give her a few minutes to decide and then make my way north.

The car I found didn't show any signs of forced entry, so it could be a coincidence, but it seems unlikely. I didn't have time or space to tell her where to go after getting here, so I hope she's waiting, somewhere.

The highway below is empty, no cars coming from either direction. A rustling from the right, leaves swishing against leaves, the snap of a twig, and I turn to look. A figure rises from the undergrowth. It's her, tattered, dirty, and in need of a few baths.

"Hey there, Zero." I stay put, not approaching.

She says nothing, standing and staring as if unsure what to do, waiting for instructions.

"Can you walk over here?" Her toe must be hurting, but she's hiding it well. I almost apologize, but this isn't the time.

She takes a step, then another. A car idles down, and I glance back to see a van pull up next to our two vehicles parked on the shoulder.

"I think we need to go, Zero. Come on."

She staggers forward a few more steps. A van door opens and closes. I glance back again to see one of my scouting parties examining the scene. They're only about three quarters of a mile away, well within range of sight, sound, or smell if they pay attention. How did they find me so fast? A closer look reveals they aren't any of the people I sent out, but they're still from Costecu's nest. The implications will have to wait for another time.

Sprinting over to Zero, I grab her around the waist and fling her over my shoulder before she has time to react. "This seems to happen a lot," I say by way of apology. This time she doesn't even try to resist.

"Where are you taking me?" she asks. There is defiance in her voice, not strong, but there. If she had any energy I suspect I'd be in for a bit of a fight. She looks like she's been through hell and back, which isn't far from the truth.

"Car."

"I know that, idiot. Where after that?"

"You'll have to wait and see."

I don't have time to explain everything, because voices rise along the highway, and then a car engine starts up. I grab the driver's-side door of my SUV, toss her into the passenger seat, and heave myself behind the wheel. She yelps. Damn. She must've hit a wound when I tossed her, but she's tough.

I floor it, tires skidding off the gravel and onto the blacktop. I keep the headlights off, not needing them for myself. It might not matter much, depending who's following us, but it can't hurt. Maybe they didn't see it was me, or maybe they don't realize what's going on, so I don't need to tempt fate by making it easier for them.

Zero struggles upright into her seat and buckles the seatbelt. "Are you going to help me or kill me?"

The question is so blunt I can't contain my laughter. "Why would I do all this if I was going to kill you?"

"Because you're a sick fuck."

I can't help myself. Teasing her is so much fun, whether I'm doing it for a reason or for pure entertainment. Her reactions are so perfect. "Don't go acting like you don't like it, Zero."

She grunts and turns her head to look out the window at the dark shapes moving past in the dark night.

Keeping watch for the pursuers via the rearview mirror, I allow myself to indulge in some private admiration. She's survived everything that's been thrown at her, which is pretty amazing. There were so many times I figured she would give up, but she hasn't. Even now, I wonder what she'd do if I pressed her hard. Fight, for all the good it would do, but it's the thought that counts.

It doesn't seem like anyone is following us. Either they decided we weren't a problem, they got lost, or they're being sneaky. I doubt it's the latter. No one's ever been sneaky, preferring the direct approach of chasing and hitting. To be fair, I helped foster the violent attitude.

"Where are we going?" she asks again, persistent as a kitten with a string.

"Somewhere safe."

"You're not going to tell me."

"Is it important?" I keep my eyes fixed on the road ahead. With no sign of anyone behind us I flick on the headlights, just in case. We don't need to get pulled over.

"I'd like to know if we're going to your murder cabin, so yes. I need to prepare."

"In fact, it is my cabin," I admit, the need to reassure her too strong to resist. "But there won't be any murder taking place there."

She grunts again. I'm not sure how to take it—resigned or expectant. Silence descends in the vehicle, but the tension radiating from her fills the space like a scratchy blanket. If it was able to speak it would say things like "I think I'm going to die," and "I don't trust this guy with my life," which is strange because she *is* trusting me with her life. I get the feeling she could fling herself out the door or into my arms. The uncertainty is enough to leave an edge crawling across my nerves.

It's a full thirty more minutes to the exit, and then another five along a county road before I turn off onto a gravel path, which is unbelievably, a real road. The gravel gives way to dirt.

"This isn't creepy," she says, voice flat.

"You don't think a getaway to a secluded cabin, free from all the tethers of modern technology and society where you can be yourself is romantic?"

She turns to glare at me, fierce in the darkness, but says nothing. I wish I knew what was going on behind those sharp green eyes.

"If I had my choice, I'd be on a beach," she says. "And there wouldn't be any killers."

I raise my eyebrows but leave her alone. After a few more bumpy minutes I pull to a stop in front of a rusted cattle gate and turn to fix her with a look. "I'm going to open it up. Stay here."

"Where would I go? You'd catch me in five seconds."

"Exactly." The air outside is cool, and smells of trees and moss. An owl hoots, calling for friends or territory. The only other sound is my footsteps on the dirt, the snapping of a twig. The gate isn't locked—it's more for show than anything else, and I drag it open with a creak, then head back to the SUV. Zero's gaze follows me every step of the way until I'm back in my seat.

"Miss me?" I ask with a winning smile.

"Not for one second."

"Aw, Zero. It's not attractive when you lie."

We bump and bounce our way along the dirt track for another five minutes, rattling all the thoughts out of my skull and leaving no room for conversation. Around a bend, surrounded by trees, the cabin comes into view.

It's not dilapidated, only a little unused. The previous owner kept good care of it. The outside is suitably rustic, a one-story affair with a peaked roof and impeccable corners. A large porch greets visitors and leads them to the door.

"See? Not creepy at all," I say, gesturing.

Her monosyllabic reply doesn't give me much to work with. I open my door and walk around the SUV to open her door. She sits and stares at me, arms crossed, one eyebrow up.

"Something on your mind?"

"I'm trying to figure out if I trust you," she says, still assessing me as if she's reading my history printed inside my skull.

"You got in the SUV."

"You grabbed me and threw me into it."

"You could have resisted."

"Would it have mattered?"

"No." I smile.

"So why waste my energy?" It's almost as if she's asking for permission to give up. I don't really want her to give up.

"Are you going to resist now?" My smile grows wider. I hope she does.

"No, but I don't need your help." She turns in the seat and glares at me until I move aside, then steps down to the dirt.

"You don't have any shoes," I point out.

She ignores me and walks to the porch. I follow, watching her butt, and then her feet as she tries to hide the limp. Ignoring the spike of guilt at the injury, I step around her, pull out my keys, and unlock the door, stepping inside first on the off chance someone unhappy with me is waiting to attack.

Everything is dark and quiet inside. I point to the couch in front of the stone fireplace, empty and hungry for logs. "Sit while I turn on the electricity."

I don't wait to see if she does, but I hear the creak of springs before I head through the kitchen into the utility room. Everything looks undisturbed if a bit dusty. I flip the main breaker, and no lights come on because I turned them all off before I left last time. A flick of the switch turns the kitchen lights on, and the living area light comes on after, hanging from the ceiling.

Zero is sitting on the couch, back to me. The tension in her shoulders is apparent. Her long, black hair is a tangled mess, yet I still want to run my fingers through it.

I move around the side, pulling the chain to turn on the lamp sitting on the end table. Everything in the living room is some shade of calming brown, from the dark wood floors to the copper lamp. When a fire is lit the whole room glows in warmth.

My footsteps are muffled by the thick area rug, which could use a vacuuming. It's been a few months since I was here, and the air has the stale smell of an unlived-in place. I drop into the big leather chair, perfect for my frame, sitting at a right angle to the couch. Zero looks at me out of the corner of her eye.

She's really dirty. Her face is smudged with dirt, her previously white top is streaked with more dirt, and the cuff of her pants are covered in mud from sitting in the bushes. There's a leaf in her hair. "You're filthy."

"You sure know how to make a woman feel good," she says, crossing her arms over her chest.

I can't help but notice how it makes her breasts move. Having her here in my cabin, which I rarely use, feels like she's sitting in my home and we're about to have coffee, followed by sex. Evil Drew is sitting up and paying attention.

"What I mean is, would you like to shower?" I tilt my head in the direction of the bathroom. "The water will be hot soon."

She stares at me, her gaze fixed on mine, unwavering. I don't flinch.

"Do you have any food while we wait?"

"I'm sure there's something in the pantry. Nothing frozen or cold." I'm sure to keep my muscles relaxed, face neutral, and don't betray one bit of the excitement within my chest. That's as close to acceptance as she's displayed yet.

"I'm pretty hungry." Her fingers drum on her forearm, little flashes of color on her nails wiggling like fish in a tank.

"Okay." I push up and walk into the kitchen, throwing a quick glance over my shoulder as I reach the door, but she's not looking at me. She's staring into the empty fireplace.

The pantry reveals some boxes of snack crackers, canned vegetables and soup, and moldy bread. I grab the unopened box of Wheat Thins and check the expiration date. Still a couple months left, so they'll be good. Stopping at the cabinets to grab a glass and fill it with water, I walk back into the living room and set down the box of crackers to fish out a coaster for the glass of water.

"You use coasters?" she asks, which is not a question I expected.

"Of course. I don't want to ruin the finish. I'm not a barbarian. Do you want some soup? I have tomato and cream of mushroom."

"This is fine," she says, grabbing the box and ripping the top open like a hungry dog. The crinkle of plastic is like a firecracker in the quiet of the room. The snap of the crackers between her teeth are like gunshots. She doesn't look at me as she chews with determination.

The swoop of her jaw draws my attention like a magnet. The way it moves as she chews is hypnotic. Her fingers hold each wheat square by the corner, popping them into her mouth at a rapid pace.

"Slow down. You'll give yourself a stomachache if you eat too fast."

She jerks her head up to focus on me as if she'd forgotten I was there. "Don't you have something better to do?"

"Not really." I could make sure the bedroom is set up, but I'd rather sit here and watch her.

Her eyes narrow and she twists away a little, tucking the box out of sight. She does slow down her chewing, only pausing to gulp half the glass of water. I rest my hands on my knees and look at her feet. The injured one is still swollen, the toe and surrounding area are red. It's a wonder she's been able to walk on it this whole time.

Her white top leaves her arms enticingly uncovered, and my gaze glides down to her hands. No rings or bracelets obstruct my view of her wrists and fingers, but she does have small studs for earrings.

She clears her throat. I've been caught, but play it off with a smirk. "Enjoying the view, Zero."

"Creep," she mutters, frowning.

"You look much prettier when you smile."

"Jesus," she rolls her eyes and turns back to face me, angry. "Can't you be a normal person? I'm not your girlfriend. I don't even trust you. Treat me like an adult, please."

"Then why are you here?"

"Like I had a choice," she says, delicious eyebrows wrenching down even further. She's glaring at me, but all I see is a furious kitten. Lots of noise and teeth, but harmless.

"You always have a choice. Life is full of choices."

"Oh yeah? Was your choice to work for Costecu, and your choice to torture me?"

"Yes," I shrug, not trying to avoid anything. "I do what I have to do."

"Why? Why do you have to do stuff like that?" She closes the box with a snap as the tab slides into the slot. She's staring at me with an intensity that's trying to unearth all my secrets.

I clench my jaw and glare back at her. "That's not your business, Zero. You should shower now."

"Smooth segue." She chews on her upper lip, face softening into thought for a few seconds before speaking again. "Fine."

I'm surprised she let the subject drop, but like the old saying goes, don't look a gift selkie in the mouth. I push up from the chair, a little creak from the old leather under my hands accentuating the silent gaze she's leveling at me. "Can you walk?"

"Of course I can walk. I'm not crippled." She stands, reaches to grab the glass of water, and drinks the rest of it. It pains me because I won't be able to stare at her backside, but I go first. Down the hallway opposite the kitchen are the doors for the two bedrooms and the bathroom. One bedroom on the left, one on the right, and the bathroom at the end of the hall. The door is hanging open a little, so I push it the rest of the way and turn on the light.

"Costecu pays really well," she says behind me.

"I didn't buy this," I reply, turning sideways to let her pass in the small hall. After a second of me not moving while she stares, she also turns sideways and sidles past. Her breath tickles my beard. I could lean forward and push her against the wall. Her softness would feel good against me. I don't do anything and she turns away as she enters the room.

"There aren't any towels."

"I'll get some."

I leave her examining the sink and shower to grab some towels out of the closet in the bedroom to the left. When I come back she's staring at herself in the mirror, hands gripping the lip of the sink. As I reach around the wall to hang up the towels, she turns to look at me.

"Don't you dare peek."

"Wouldn't dream of it."

She snorts and rolls her eyes. "Go away now."

"I'll be right out there, reading a book."

"You can read?" The snark rolls off her tongue like water.

"Careful, Zero," I say, snatching her smug chin and holding tight. "You keep poking and you're going to get bit."

She holds my gaze, unwavering, and after a few seconds I drop my hand. The short walk back to the living room might as well be a thousand miles. Leaving her behind in the bathroom goes against all my instincts, as well as my desire. The door clicks, and I settle into the couch, open the drawer of the side table, and pull out the book I'd been reading the last time I was here.

The tap squeaks, the water starts, and the door clicks open on its own. It never did stay shut. I eye the gap. Tempting movement, shadows, and light flicker in the room, but there's no way to tell what's going on. It doesn't affect me any less, though.

Is that a flash of white? The sound of cloth on skin? A small clunk as the glass shower door shuts, and now she's in the shower, under the water. Wet and dripping, all the dirt running down her skin and into the drain.

I keep my promise not to peek, because one thing she didn't seem to remember is she doesn't have any other clothes to wear. I'm looking forward to seeing her wrapped in a towel.

I laugh to myself, turn my attention back to the book, and wait.

CHAPTER SEVENTEEN

Aideen

I toss my clothes on the floor, open the shower door, and step in. The water isn't quite to the temperature I want, but it's warm, and it's heaven. I stand under the stream as it heats up to hot, letting the past days flow off of me with all the dirt, dried blood, and grime.

It all swirls down the drain, the water going from clear to brick brown, and then diluting to a hazy tinge of hard water. I turn around to let the heat caress my back and work the fingers of my uninjured hand into the hopeless nest of my hair. It's a nasty mess, but I knew that from looking in the mirror.

My whole face was a mess—sunken red eyes, skin paler than normal, and dirt everywhere. It looked like I hadn't eaten in days, which my stomach agreed with. It rumbled a little in protest with the speed I'd taken down those crackers. The glass of water had been helpful, but the salt in the crackers tasted so good.

I work a knot free as the tangles disappear into smoothness and move on to another. There's a bottle of bodywash and a bottle of shampoo plus conditioner, made for guys who don't want to think about conditioner. Expensive shampoo is one thing I'm glad I've never had to worry about. All I need is a little bit of suds to get the dirt out, and the water and my selkie ancestry do the rest.

The water is doing its work. I unwrap the filthy gauze from around my fingers and toss the wet mess over the shower wall. The wooden splits fall to the floor, and I hold my hand under the water where I can see them. The itching as the fingers repair themselves the rest of the way bothers me, like it always does. It's an itch I can't scratch, one under the skin, inside the bones, but it'll only last a few minutes.

To distract myself I look at my foot instead, and with passive interest watch the missing toenail grow back and the red fade into the color of my skin. A missing toenail isn't an injury I've suffered before, and I'm not sure what else I expected to happen, but it feels anti-climactic. Another few seconds and the swelling is gone.

I flex my previously broken fingers. All seems to be in working order, and the weird tickle is already fading. A wave of exhaustion sweeps over me, typical to the healing process, and I lean against the cold tiles to shock myself back awake. Almost there. I need to get sort of clean and then I can go to sleep.

At this point I'm not sure if I care whether I wake up again. Sheets and a mattress and a real pillow will feel like such a luxury. It's ages and a life ago I slept in my own bed.

Grabbing the bottle of shampoo and squirting a bunch on my hand, I attack my hair with purpose. Scrubbing hard, using my fingers to get deep, the rest of the snarls release back into my natural straight black tresses.

The water turns dark from the accumulated dust and dirt, soap bubbles floating on the top of the sludge, but slowly turns back to regular water as I keep scrubbing. Another palmful of white goo finishes the job from roots to tips.

A loofah hangs from the single knob controlling water temperature, and I wrinkle my nose at it. The phrase *I don't know where that's been* isn't applicable since I know exactly where it's been, and I don't want it touching me.

Hands it is.

The bodywash has a scent the bottle describes as "Ocean." I'm not sure what "Ocean" is supposed to smell like, but this smells like chemical salt and some type of flower. Why does a dwarf use a scent from a tropical island?

I'm not as thorough as I should be, but I also don't care as much as I should. I'll settle for seventy-five percent clean, because the exhaustion is creeping back and another press against the tiles doesn't help much. A quick survey of my body to search for anything abnormal reveals nothing but bits of dirt, and then I can't wait anymore. I shut off the water.

I squeeze out my hair in a rush, feeling the bed calling, and reach out to grab a white towel. It wraps up my black locks, and then the other dries me off. They're fluffy, but stiff as if they haven't been used in a while, and a faint smell of dust floats around before being battered away by coconut.

As I step onto the rug, I notice the door cracked open. That fucker. I'm too tired to do anything about it now, but he's going to pay tomorrow. Then my eyes hit my clothes. They're ruined. Not even a professional cleaner could get them back to a wearable state, and even if they could, I don't think I'd want to put them on ever again. Too many intense and painful memories are tied up in them. It wouldn't be good for my psyche.

I have nothing to wear.

I re-tuck the towel around me. It's large, but not big enough for my comfort, exposing half my thighs along with all the rest of my legs. Well aware of how I almost glow after a shower or bath, every imperfection eased out by the cleansing water, I chew my lip. I'm not giving Lindberg something else to be lewd about. I stare at the gap in the door like it's responsible for this, not having anywhere safe to express my anger.

That last second, when he'd grabbed me by my chin, had turned my guts to jelly. In that moment he'd dropped his fake and playful exterior, and I saw the anger simmering behind his eyes. I'd used all my willpower not to look away from him. Perhaps being exposed to it when he was locked behind glass had given me some immunity, but it was still terrifying.

Then the casual façade returned, and he was back to the dwarf who pretended like nothing bothered him. Though I tell myself I'm crazy, I kind of want to keep poking and see if he's all bark and no bite. I need to know who he is.

I hope he's not as creepy as I've been proclaiming. I crack the door open a bit more.

"Hey." It's half a question, half a statement, and half tentative.

Leather creaks and steps get louder as they come closer. I push the door shut a bit more and hide behind it.

"Yes, Zero?" he asks, using the name I've heard so much I almost don't hate it. It helps to think someone named Zero went through all the trauma, and not me, Aideen Duffy.

"I don't have anything to wear." It's an innocent enough confession, because really, what would I have to wear? But my cheeks heat up anyway. It's not like he can see through the door and the towel, so it shouldn't fluster me as much as it does.

"I gave you towels, Zero," the rumble comes back with a hint of a laugh.

"I'm not wearing a freaking towel to bed," I hiss through my teeth. "Don't you have clothes here or something?"

"I'll see what I've got."

"Thank you."

I try not to imagine what it would've been like if I'd walked out in this. His stare would've felt like fingers. Every time he looks at me I feel heat. Letting him see this much skin would've been insane. I shiver and remember the feeling of exposing myself to cut the tracker out.

Sharp and tingly.

His footsteps come back and he nudges at the door enough to shove a large hand through. "Here."

I snatch the shirt. It's a button-down, of course, a deep blue with little white polka-dots in a regular pattern. It looks pretty good, in fact. I never really stopped to think about it, but he's always been dressed impeccably.

"This is it?" I ask through the door instead of complimenting his fashion sense.

"Sorry, all my nightgowns are at the cleaners, and I don't think my pants will fit you."

"You're not funny."

"Take it or leave it." The footsteps clomp back to the living room before I can mount any further protest.

I scowl, push the door shut with a click, and when it pops up by itself, I push it closed again and look around for something to jam against it and keep it closed. Maybe he didn't come and look. Not able to think of anything else, I drop my towel on the floor and shove it against the door. It holds it closed.

Avoiding eye contact in the mirror, I pull on the shirt, and button it up all the way, and only then do I look. It's big, and if I was any less than the height I am it would be too big. It's long enough to at least cover the same length as the towel did, with the added comfort of not coming undone at the slightest touch. The sleeves need to be rolled up to free my hands.

I look ridiculous with it buttoned all the way up to my chin. Undoing the first button looks better, but his shoulders are so broad and the neckline so wide it shows a good deal of my collarbone.

This is what someone would wear after sleeping with the owner of the shirt. The thought causes an uncomfortable little tremor in my stomach. I'm not going to sleep with him, and no one is going to see me wearing this, so it doesn't matter.

I catch myself rubbing my hip and stop.

He's not going to see me in it anyway, since I'm going to flee into a bedroom and go to sleep. I open the door a tiny bit.

"Close your eyes," I whisper. Why am I whispering? I repeat the request at full volume.

"I'm reading my book," he says.

"Which bedroom can I use?" I'm stalling.

"Whichever one you want."

"If you try to have sex with me, I'll seriously kill you."

"Wouldn't dream of it." Whatever note he hits with the word "dream" makes my insides tremor again.

I open the door and step out, only to find him sitting on the chair and staring right at me. I yelp in anger and shock, and scurry into the bedroom with the open door, then slam it behind me. My face is heated down to my neck, and I'm pissed. I crack the door open.

"You said you wouldn't look," I shout.

"No, I didn't. I said I'm reading my book."

"Bastard."

"It looks good on you, Zero. You ought to wear my clothes more often." He's laughing, I can hear it clear as day. He's laughing at me and imagining me in his clothes.

"What the fuck is wrong with you?"

Footfall approaches, and his voice gets closer with every word. "You think it's wrong for a man to want to look at a beautiful woman? You think it's wrong for me to look at *you*?" The last word is said inches from me as he comes to a stop on the other side of the door.

"Yes," I croak, all the moisture having fled my mouth. His breathing is low and steady, his presence a physical force. He's blocking almost all the light from the living room.

"You think it's wrong for me to imagine what I want to do with you?" It's not menacing, and it's not loud, but it's said with determination as large as a mountain.

The tremors have moved to places besides my stomach. I don't shut the door all the way, even though it wouldn't do any good. The certainty he could break it down in a flick of his wrist and there's not a damn thing I could do about it nestles in my heart. Despite myself, I ask the question, voice low and halting. "What do you want to do with me?"

In the pause I'm sure the world has stopped, or maybe exploded. The wait is excruciating. I shuffle my feet and clamp my legs together to try to stop the rising fire. This is crazy. I don't know why I'm reacting this way, but I don't like it, yet I want more.

"I want to make sure you get a good night's sleep, and then breakfast in the morning. You're exhausted."

I blink. Cold water douses the heat simmering in my brain, and the spell is broken.

"Oh. Good," I mumble. "Good, yes, because I need sleep. I'm tired."

"I'm sure you are." He sounds so reasonable. His voice isn't resonating in any sort of primal timbre, it's a normal voice.

It was silly to get so worked up. I'm tired, that's all it is. He's a killer, a dangerous and possibly psychotic murderer. I'm not even safe here. "I am."

"You should go to bed."

"I will."

"Goodnight, Zero." The footsteps fade back to the other room.

"Goodnight," I whisper to nobody.

I close the door.

The moon provides enough light to see the room after my eyes adjust to the dark. The decor is sparse, a queen bed with a nightstand on either side, each with its own lamp. A dresser stands open with clothes hanging off the hangers. There's not much else.

The sheets feel clean, though they smell stale like everything else here. The pillows are firm. I slip under the sheets, pull the towel off my head, and lay back, staring at the ceiling. Everything smells subtly like Lindberg.

No doubt it's the shirt. Even though he hasn't worn it in whatever amount of time, I can still tell it's his. The fabric is soft. It must have cost at least a couple hundred dollars. Where does he get the money, and what did he mean when he said he didn't buy the cabin?

Thoughts like that distract me from the questions I should be asking, like if I'm going to be alive in the morning, and have I lost my damn mind?

I'm going to fall asleep in a cabin in the middle of nowhere with a man in the next room who's broken my fingers and didn't even apologize for it.

In his shirt. After using his shampoo.

I try to squirm into a more comfortable position, but changing the way I lie doesn't ease the burr in my brain.

I jerk awake, not realizing I'd drifted off, at a thump coming from somewhere else in the cabin. Colorful curses, muffled by the walls, reach my ears. For some reason it's comforting. He probably dropped something. He's a person. A very large, sometimes angry person, with a super nice beard and really strong hands. Right? I'm sure it's fine. He's not going to come in here and ravage me. The door isn't going to burst open, and I won't be taken like an animal. Right?

I stare at the door until I fall asleep.

CHAPTER EIGHTEEN

Druain

I sit in the chair for a while and try to read the book, but I can't focus. Zero is in the other room, the room I use, sleeping in my bed in my shirt. Nothing on the pages could compete with my imagination of what's at hand.

A few steps, an easy push on the door, and there she'd be. Buttons wouldn't stand a chance, and the shirt doesn't matter more than what it's hiding.

Seeing a peek of her panties in the SUV was one thing, but it took all my strength not to stare at her chest the whole time she was out here. My oversized shirt isn't enough to hide the hints of her breasts.

More than her body, which is a great body from what I've been able to see, I want to understand how she's so mentally strong. Not once have I felt she's been afraid, and often I've felt she was in my head with me, sorting through my thoughts.

After another fifteen minutes of trying to fight it, I get up and head to the bathroom. The sad pile of her clothes lay in the corner. I pick up the pants and top. They're disgusting, covered in mud and dried blood. If it were up to me I'd take them in back and burn them, but I don't want to leave the house yet. I attempt to wash them in the sink since I don't have detergent for the washing machine, then I wring them out in the shower and hang them from the towel rack.

That leaves her underwear, lying on the floor. Items I shouldn't be looking at. Evil Drew grumbles and paces. I take a few breaths in and out. What the hell, she's asleep, they need cleaning, it's not like I'm doing anything weird. I'm cleaning up.

They're green. Of course, they're green. They were green the other day, and it's not like she's been able to change. I pick up the bra first. A little fringe of lace along the top edges of the cups adds some fanciness, but otherwise it's sensible. Not flashy or meant to show off, only enough to perform a job. I toss it in the sink.

Looping a pinky through the band of the panties, I lift them up. They're a bit lacy, but still practical. I hold them for longer than I should before putting them in the sink as well. Hot water and hand soap washes everything. I hope it doesn't ruin them.

They get hung up along with her clothes and I manage to walk out of the bathroom. The door to her bedroom is shut, and there's only silence inside, which doesn't stop me from pausing for a minute.

My stomach growls, snapping me out of the daze. I find my hand on the doorknob and pull it back. I need to get food for her. She can't eat only soup and crackers. A few minutes of hesitation at leaving her alone leaves me frustrated. When did making decisions get so hard? She's fine, no one's coming, and she's asleep.

I almost slam the door behind me on the way out, remembering to not wake her up. I get in the SUV and drive off. There's a Walmart about forty-five minutes north where I can pick up groceries. It doesn't have to be much, supplies for a few days while I figure out where to stash her permanently.

The ride is dark and quiet with no one to tease and no scent to fill the other side. I turn on the radio and then turn it off five minutes later. Politics and sports are such minor things, and the music is pretty bad. The clock reads one am in light blue.

The occasional flash of a car coming the other way is the only sign I'm not alone on this night. I find my thoughts drifting back to Zero, alone. No one knows where the cabin is, or even that I have it, but it's still unsettling to leave her alone.

The lights of the town creep over the horizon, and soon enough I'm parked and striding into the bright white lights of convenience. The cart wheel rattles, like they always do, as I make my way up and down aisles in the mostly deserted grocery section. The only people awake at this time on a weekday night are druggies and teenagers—sometimes the same person.

As I'm looking through the glass in the frozen food section, trying to decide what type of pizza Zero might like, I catch a glimpse of my reflection. The shirt I'm wearing still has a splash of blood on it, which would explain why the guy with meth pockmarks turned around and ran away. I shrug and pick a pepperoni pizza. Can't go wrong with pepperoni, unless she's a vegetarian. If she's *vegan*, I'm truly fucked. What's the category where they won't eat animal products, but will eat fish? I hope she eats meat.

Just in case, I grab some vegetables then stare at my eclectic haul. Bottled water, several types of chips, the frozen pizza along with chicken nuggets and mozzarella sticks, two types of cereal, milk, cookie dough as well as chocolate chip ice cream, and two tomatoes, a head of lettuce, and a cucumber. I better get salad dressing.

The self-checkout lanes aren't open this late. The only open lane has a group of kids in it trying to buy cigarettes. The clerk is adamant they need ID, and they keep getting more and more belligerent. Not wanting to stand around forever while Zero's all by herself, I walk around my cart and loom, waiting for them to notice. It only takes a couple of moments.

"Why don't you go home to your parents and your bunk beds?"

They eye me, then as a group turn and run off. There are perks to being huge and scary.

The clerk goes to thank me, and then his eyes fix on the blood.

"I hit a deer," I say. It's an awful excuse, but it must give him a bit of peace, because he nods and rings me up. The chime of each barcode is the countdown to me getting back to Zero. I pay in cash, leave the cart behind, and carry the bags to the SUV.

The drive back is longer than the drive there, and several times I catch myself going ninety. Slowing down to ten above the speed limit is torture, but I didn't get where I am by being reckless. Being pulled over by some overzealous cop would only make things worse.

I pull to a stop in front of the tube gate, hop out to open it, and ice crashes into my lungs. I didn't close the gate when I left. I left it open because no one ever comes here.

A quick dash to the SUV to turn it and the lights off, and darkness falls again. I stand, listening, waiting, scanning for any sign of something out of place, some mark people are here. It might have been the wind, it might have been Zero, but I'm not taking chances.

Nothing breaks the silence, so I walk up the dirt road toward the cabin. I take a few steps past the gate before slipping into the woods on the left side. Slow and careful, watching for leaves, rocks, and sticks, I creep forward, keeping the road to my right. There's still no sign of anyone, and no sounds except the night creatures.

Halfway there, voices reach my ears and I pause, bringing my feet into a steady stance, ready for anything. Quiet voices, but voices nonetheless. Two, maybe three, talking in hushed tones, slightly above a whisper. I can't make out words yet, but if I can hear them, they'll be able to hear me. I move forward, slower, angling a bit further into the woods.

Through the trees I can make out a vehicle. It's hard to get a good look, but it appears to be the one from the highway. Did they follow me and I didn't notice, or did they find this place by accident? I can't imagine them waiting the hours until I left, and even then I've been gone over an hour. They would have done something if they'd known.

Maybe they don't know Zero is in there. After all, my car wasn't there, so they might think no one's home. So then how would they figure out this is even my place? These are all great questions for which I plan to get answers.

Crouching, close to the earth and the smell of moss and insects, I weave between the trees. Step after careful step until I can see the porch. Three people are there, ones I recognize from their faces but not their names. A henchman, an underling, and a minion. Scum who delight in spreading terror or hurting innocents.

I don't get any joy from hurting people. Not innocent people, anyway. I'll take some joy from this. I keep sneaking around the side of the cabin, watching them out of the corner of my eye in case they decide to do something.

The orange glow of a cigarette lights up, then another. If I'd caught them smoking back at the base I'd give them a lecture. Cancer can get anyone—human, vampire, goblin, it doesn't matter. But it won't be a problem for them anymore.

As I'm nearing the corner one breaks off. I freeze, one hand in the dirt, knees bent, staring. He moves along the porch, saying something over his shoulder, then jumps the railing. A real badass. I watch him as he moves around the side of the building, sauntering, swinging his arm with the cigarette in it. The smoke trails up, twisting and twirling, also stinking. Helpful to cover scents.

I shadow him from the woods, using his steps to mask the sound of my own. He studies the logs of the cabin with disinterest, stops to look in a dark and empty window, then continues on. He's going to go around back, and keeps peeking in windows, and then he's going to see Zero and things will get hairy. I can't let that happen.

Taking the risk of speeding up, I stalk closer to the edge of the woods, keeping up with him as he makes the shorter trip around the cabin. He rounds the corner, heading toward the back. The front porch is out of sight, and I count to five, then scuttle forward and peek around the corner. He's still ambling, not paying attention. He looks in another window. Two more and he'll be at hers. I wish I'd bought curtains, but who would be out here to look in?

I take a breath. He turns back the other way. Four quick steps are impossible to muffle, but I clamp my hand around his mouth, grab the top of his head, and wrench. The satisfying crunch is quiet in the night, a little sound that won't be noticed with all the insects and birds.

The dirt under my feet is soft as I lower the body to the ground. No need to hide it yet. I wait, regulating my breathing down from its elevated level. Nothing to be excited about here.

I could make a pun, something like "I told you smoking would kill you," but there's no one around to hear it, and that's a horrible pun anyway. The bit of adrenaline is expected and normal. Handling it is secondhand. Slow breaths, and a moment to relax.

The murmur of conversation has ceased. They're either bored or suspicious, and again I wonder what they're waiting for. No reason for me to wait, though. I can take two at once easily. The only reason I didn't go after all three at once is because I need the energy to walk back and put away the groceries.

I go around the house the opposite way I came, another bit of precaution. As I pass Zero's window I peek inside. She's still asleep, lying on her side, a splash of black hair against the pillow. I move on before I get too caught up and stare at her all night.

The woods are closer to this side of the house, but venturing into them might cause too much noise in the sticks and leaves. I stick close to the wall, sliding around the ninety-degree angle. I move up to peek around the front corner to the porch. The henchmen are still there, idling and not talking.

There's not a lot of cover, and they'd spot me if I approached and they turned around. I'm not sure I'm quiet enough to sneak all the way up there. Confidence it is.

I break cover and stride toward the porch. After a few seconds, they turn to look at me, perhaps expecting their comrade, and when they see it's not him, they tense up. Tension dissolves into recognition and relaxation before swinging back to tension. They don't trust me. It's plain on their faces.

By the time they've gone through all those emotions, I'm up on the steps and grabbing them by the shoulders. The struggle is brief, though loud, and one of them manages to slam me against the wall. I let loose a series of curses and clobber him in the side of the head. He drops like a rock. The other is on me in an instant, but a knee to some soft parts ends the fight quick enough.

Grabbing him from behind, arm looping around his neck, I squeeze to let him know I mean business.

"How did you get here?" I growl into his ear.

He grabs at me with his free hand, but he might as well be attacking me with Marshmallow fluff for all I care. I squeeze a bit more.

"Drove," he says, some defiance still in his voice.

"Obviously, idiot. How did you find me?"

"Costecu…gave us directions."

How does Costecu know where this is? A million ways and reasons for how he shouldn't have a clue about my cabin flash through my mind. This guy won't have any answers. He was told to go somewhere and kill someone, that's it.

"Why are you here?"

"He thought..." He pauses to breathe, "You had the selkie."

"He doesn't know for sure?" I give him another squeeze to help the questioning along.

"No," he grunts. "Let me go and I won't tell him."

"Yeah, you won't." Enough pressure and he passes out, and a little more and a little longer and he won't breathe again. The struggles of the body aren't enough to stop me. It's nothing new.

I stand up, taking a breather. A few minutes later my pulse has slowed back to normal. It's worrying I'm so used to this, but I have been for a while, and nothing's going to change.

One by one I drag the bodies back to the SUV they came in, propping one in the front seat and two in the back. I have to do a complex maneuver to get around my own SUV before driving away from the cabin.

Five miles back down the state highway, at a sharp turn with a drop-off, I make a U-turn and park, pull one of the bodies out of the back and stuff him in the driver's seat, and engage the emergency brake.

Searching around the drop, I find a decent-sized rock. The metal guardrail takes a bit of work to loosen, but I don't have to do it all the way. Back at the SUV, I release the brake, drop the rock on the pedal, and jump back as the SUV jumps forward, collides with the ineffective guardrail, and disappears over the side.

A few seconds later a satisfying crash echoes from below. It doesn't explode, because this is real life, not a movie, but a quick peek shows it's mangled and broken, upside down. A body is a few feet away. This might not deter or delay Costecu for long, but it should buy me a day or two to figure out where to take Zero next.

The walk back is too long, about forty-five minutes. Halfway there I remember I left the frozen food in the SUV. A long, loud, and soothing burst of profanity makes me feel better. Small animals run away in the woods. A car passes, whipping past and not stopping, the taillights angry and judgmental.

Turning back onto my little road, I get to the SUV, close the gate this time, drive it the short distance up to the cabin, and park. The groceries are hauled inside and put away. Peeking in one of the ice cream tubs, I see it's only a little melted. Thank goodness for fall weather. I even steal a spoonful.

Fatigue is hitting me hard now. It's been over two days, and with only a restless nap in the middle of all of this, I'm about to fall over. A quick shower helps wake me up for a few minutes, enough to dry off and sneak into Zero's room to rummage in my closet and get dressed in clean clothes.

She's still sound asleep. Her breathing is measured and steady. She's lying on her stomach. The blanket has dropped down from her back, showing my shirt resting against her skin. The collar is pulled down from the back of her neck, and it's so tempting to reach out and sweep my fingers across the soft skin there. I don't.

Closing the door behind me, I struggle to the couch and flop down. I need to be out here in case she gets up. Or if anyone tries to come in, I'll be right here and ready. I should've brought a TV out here.

I stare at the door, my eyes itchy, willing myself to stay awake.

CHAPTER NINETEEN

Aideen

I wake with a start, sun hitting my face in an unfamiliar way. It all comes flooding back in an instant—the escape, the drive, Drew, the shower. I'm in his bed, the sun is shining through because there are no curtains, and I'm hungry as anything, a typical response to my healing process.

Lying there for a few minutes to absorb everything around me, listening, feeling, even a sniff or two, I get used to my surroundings. The cabin is quiet, the quiet of emptiness, the only sounds coming from outside. Soft calls of morning birds attempt to lull me into peace, but I need to get up and look around.

Sliding out from underneath the sheets, my bare feet hit the floor. The touch of unfamiliar cloth against my skin reminds me I'm not in my own clothes. Absently rubbing my hands across the sides, then fingering the buttons as I pad around the room, I take in the details I couldn't see last night.

It's clean, not a thing out of place, even though there is a thin coat of dust on everything, clearly, the cabin had not been used in a while. It's spartan, too, with the only decorations being the lamps and a single framed photo of a waterfall, the type you'd buy at a dollar store or maybe for a couple hundred bucks.

The large standing dresser in the corner is odd, until I notice there's no closet. Not a design choice I would have made, but you can't account for everyone's tastes. It has a couple drawers on the bottom and then two large doors which swing open to reveal hanging shirts on one side and slacks on the other. I sort through them, not sure what I'm looking for. Everything in the dresser is high-end, bought with blood money, no doubt.

Not able to delay any longer, I grab the brass knob of the door and twist, pulling the door open slowly, listening for any creaks it might make. It moves on the hinges without a sound, smooth and easy. I peek out, getting my bearings again. Bathroom to the left, the other bedroom right across the way, and the hall to the living area to the right. The bathroom door is open as I left it, and the other bedroom door is shut. I still don't hear anything.

Moving as quietly as I can, I step down the hallway, but only make it two steps before I see him. Drew, sitting in the chair, his back to me. I freeze, sure he must be able to hear me no matter how quiet I am, but he doesn't move. As I stare, I notice his head is tipped forward a little, and the quiet breathing seems to be the repose of sleep.

Starting forward again, heart beating faster, I creep up on him. I lick my lips as I pause behind the chair. He hasn't moved an inch. A couple more slow and soft steps leading with my toes takes me around to the side, and then I can see his eyes are closed. The slow rise and fall of his chest confirms he's asleep.

With a rush, the decision pounces on me. This is my chance to get away. Find some better clothes, no matter how poorly they fit, get some shoes, and get the heck out of here. I can make my way back—to where? To my apartment, back to headquarters. There must be some explanation for what went on there. If I walk in during the day, with all sorts of normal people around, I can get some answers. They aren't going to shoot me in the middle of downtown with hundreds of people in the building. It's got to be safer than hanging around here. He hasn't done anything yet, but it doesn't mean he won't. No doubt he's done this to tons of women, bringing them to the middle of nowhere so he can torture them in peace.

I back up the way I came, my hands behind me to make sure I don't bump anything, and then when I feel I'm at a safe distance I turn. The first thing I do is check out the second bedroom. The door opens as smoothly as mine, and there's another standing dressing there, which is filled with more clothes. Shirts and slacks, same as the other. How many shirts and slacks does one person need, and why so many in a seldom-used cabin?

In the end, I keep the shirt I've already got. There's no point in changing into another one since they're all the same size, and I'm not too worried about style at the moment. A random pair of slacks are too big, like they all would be, and a belt I dig out of one of the drawers is also too big. I double it back on itself through the buckle and cinch it tight, then roll up the cuffs, which matches what I did with the sleeves. I don't need a mirror to know I look ridiculous, like a kid in adult clothes.

I find his shoes tucked underneath the bed, and with a few socks shoved in they don't fall off as soon as I walk, which is the most I can hope for. Then I take them off because there's no way I can walk quietly with them on, and carry them with me.

Sitting on the edge of the bed and peeling off one of the pairs of socks I'd put on, I wonder again why I'm trying to leave. It feels obvious. Lindberg is a verified killer with more than one victim. There's no reason I should trust him. Still, there's a nagging part of my brain reminding me he did give me the message that led me here, and he did patch up my wounds. I roll my eyes. The wounds he gave me without any hesitation.

As I move across to the bathroom, I peek over at him again. Still asleep. The sight of all my clothes hanging on the towel rack is not something I expected. They're damp. He tried to clean them.

I don't get him. One second he's slapping me, breaking my fingers, and the next he's helping me escape and washing my clothes. What a strange puzzle. The urge to dive into his mind and figure it all out is overwhelming, an itch I should resist scratching. He's a killer, period. Even killers pet kittens sometimes.

I fiddle with my hair in the mirror, and search around looking for a brush, but only find a comb. It doesn't work so well in the mess my hair became, being wet and slept on. After a moment's hesitation, I use the one toothbrush available. No need to skimp on dental hygiene. It's a toothbrush.

Unsure as to why I'm stalling, I scowl at myself, take a couple more moments, and then head back into the front room. Sneaking past to the kitchen, side-eyeing Lindberg to be sure he's still asleep, beard touching his chest, I decide to ransack the kitchen for any remaining crackers.

What greets me in the refrigerator is more than soup. Grabbing the milk, angry he kept this from me, I expect it to be expired. But it's still good for a couple weeks. Checking every package and box, they're all new. He must have gone out while I was sleeping.

I look at him again over the bar counter, slumped down in the chair, and a corner of my mind pipes up: He's trying to help you, it says. He got you food, he slept out here, he's being nice.

He pulled out my toenail, the rational part of me replies. He constantly ogles me, and I'm surprised he didn't try to do something while I was sleeping.

But he didn't, the corner says, smirking.

He groped me the entire ride from headquarters, I shoot back.

You liked it.

No, I didn't.

I grab the cereal box and study it with intense focus. You'd think raisin bran would be healthy, but it has a lot of sugar, which is why I don't eat it.

Satisfied with my level of distraction, I twist two bottles of water off of the rings and nab the bag of sour cream and onion potato chips, my favorite. The crinkle as I pick it up sounds like lightning. I freeze, jaw clenched, head snapping toward him, expecting doom to come, but he doesn't even move.

After forcing my muscles to relax, one by one from my head to my toes, I sink to the floor, out of line of sight, just in case.

There's no back door. I'm going to have to get past him, open the door, and hope it doesn't make any noise either. I don't remember if it did the night before. I was too out of it to notice.

The darker wood floor is shiny and hard, which would be painful on my knees, but a quick shuffle proves I won't be able to crawl and hold my water, snack, and the shoes at the same time. I crouch at the edge of the counter, peeking around it. I can barely see the side of his face.

Time to test my leg muscles. Staying low in a crouch, each step hard but doable, I make my way across the floor, bobbing up and down with each step. Step, step, step. The floor is solid with no sign of loose boards or squeaking. This whole cabin feels expensive, and everything is solid and beautiful. I really could enjoy spending some time here, surrounded by nature, if it wasn't for all the danger the big burly dwarf would put me in.

My leg muscles are a little annoyed at me by the time I get to the door, and I make a note to work them out a bit more, but it's nothing horrible. Now that I'm at the door, and I'm reaching for the knob, once again, I wonder why I'm doing this. Why am I exchanging a bed and shower and raisin bran cereal for the unknowns of woods and whatever waits for me back in the city? If I ever get back to the city.

I look back over my shoulder at Lindberg. He's still sleeping, no sign of waking up. The knob makes the smallest of clicks as the latch disengages, but the hinges don't even creak as I pull the door open and crouch my way outside. As I shut the door with a sigh, surprise tension leaves my body, washed out of my muscles to ground into the deck.

Crouch-walking down the stairs of the porch, because I can never be too safe, I push all the doubts and questions away. No time for hesitation. It's time to get the heck out of here.

The woods are right there, and I scurry, careful as I can, to the edge of them and hide behind a tree to put on all the socks and the pair of shoes. No need to get stabbed by a rock. I've felt enough foot pain to last a lifetime.

The laces are almost new, and smooth between my fingers with the slight bit of stiffness meaning they haven't been broken in yet. Brown, like the shoes, they're not meant for walking in the woods. These are meant for walking in a coffee shop or a bookstore. He's going to be pissed when I get mud on them.

One last glance over my shoulder at the closed door, the morning sun shining on the side of the house, and the unseen occupant within. It's almost peaceful, a rustic vacation retreat for affluent people.

I've never been great with directions, but I can follow along the dirt road leading back to the state highway. I plan to stay out of sight in case anyone comes looking for me or him, as I make my way back to the city. As the morning air warms up a little, I reflect on my stupidity for trusting Lindberg and coming out here. I must've been delusional from the pain and adrenaline. Now that I feel better, I've had some sleep, and I have food and water, the situation seems a lot better.

The heft of the water bottles and the crinkle of the chip bag are comforting companions. Now I understand how people fold under pressure. The torture was horrible and painful, but the hours after, when it was over, as my body came down from all the stress, that's where he got me. His devious plan is as obvious as the moss on the trees, and I fell for it like a complete idiot. Who knows what he would have done to me in his cabin?

Feed me frozen pizza, look at me with those burning eyes, and I would have folded like his socks, neat and predictable. I open the bag of chips and munch away, wondering if he knew they were my favorite flavor or if it was a coincidence. How much information do they have on me? He kept asking for my name, but maybe it was a way to tell at what point I'd tell the truth.

The gate is closed across the road, but there's no fence so I walk past it. I've already finished the chips without realizing until I hit the bottom of the empty bag. I crumple it and shove it into the pocket of his pants, jealous about something so simple as pockets in pants.

The crack from the water bottle lid is satisfying, the snaps like popping a hundred tiny bubbles. I've taken a sip when I see the old blacktop of the state highway through the trees. A couple of steps and I'm on the edge of the small culvert. I crouch down to consider my next move. It's either go forward or go back, and there's no way I'm going back now. That would be stupid.

As I'm hunkered down and contemplating this easy decision, my overly large shoes slowly sinking into the wet earth, I miss the sound of the car until it's rounded the bend and bearing down on me. I tense, try to squish down further, then chide myself because it's only a car. Other people drive this way all the time, and there's no reason it's here for me.

Except it slows, and then it stops, and before I can get my stupid brain to believe what my eyes are telling it, the doors have opened and four people step out. It takes me a second to register how large they are—small compared to Lindberg, but they're big. Three men and a woman, and they look all business.

I can do nothing but try not to move: a tiny rabbit in the grass hoping the predatory cats don't see it, because if they do there's nowhere for me to go. It must be coincidence, I hope, I wish, they're here for something else. There's got to be something else going on, or they're changing drivers. Something. Anything.

The smallest amount of water I'd drank dries up like a puddle in the desert of my mouth. My heart is racing, struggling to get out of my chest and away from my body, which might be about to have a really bad time. The only thing I can do is stare at the tops of their heads as they walk across the pavement.

I could run. Get up and dash back off into the woods, try to get away. When they catch up, which they will, I could fight, struggle, kick, and punch, and inflict as much damage as possible. Maybe I can make enough noise Lindberg would come out and rescue me.

What an odd thought. Why would he rescue me? He's the one who called them to come here and get me. He let himself sleep because he knew I wouldn't escape, and he knew I couldn't hurt him. Another mental manipulation to show me he's in charge and I'm helpless against anything he wants to do.

I won't give him the satisfaction of being told how I struggled and fought. Imagining how they'll all laugh at me is a worse fate than almost anything else I can think up. I'll go out with dignity.

My legs still shake as I stand up, even though I've already been spotted. They aren't cats going after a rabbit, they're wolves closing in on a deer. Eyes narrowed, grins wide, and swagger in every step, one walks right up to me.

"Hey there, bitch," he says, then backhands me.

It hurts, my cheek flushing to heat from the blow, but I don't fall. "That all you got?"

This time he punches me, his fist the last thing I remember.

CHAPTER TWENTY

Druain

With a jerk I wake up. Shit, I fell asleep. Sludge clogs my muscles as I struggle out of the chair and stagger over to the bedroom and push the door open. Zero's gone. Shit. My impeccable internal clock tells me it's still morning. The light streaming through the window is another good hint. I must've slept only a handful of hours, but it was enough for her to get up and leave. Why she left is a question she'll answer when I get her back.

When I crash open the door to the other bedroom, I find the standing dresser open. Some clothes are missing, along with a lot of socks and a pair of shoes. In the kitchen a couple of bottles of water and a bag of chips are gone. Why she didn't take more is another minor mystery, but not something more worrying than her leaving.

Back into the bedroom to at least change out of my blood-stained shirt before I go charging back out into the world, I try to decide where she'd go. Back to the city, or further north along the state highway, or maybe she'd strike out west into the woods behind the cabin.

Going into the woods seems unlikely, since I don't think she has intimate knowledge of this area and doesn't seem like the type of person to wander in a random direction without a goal. She's probably headed back to the city because she thinks she can accomplish something there, which is a complete reversal of her deciding to come here. I don't understand what's going on. I thought we'd had the beginnings of an understanding, but I guess not.

Damn woman. What the hell is she thinking? She's only going to get caught. Didn't I give her protection and a safe place to sleep? Food and shelter? I killed five people trying to keep her safe, and what does she do? Runs off again. I'm going to strangle her when I find her, and I'm going to find her. I'll scour every inch of the country to track her down and bring her back to safety, whether she wants it or not.

Shoving past the chair in the living room, knocking it aside in my haste and anger, I wrench open the door and step onto the porch. The SUV is still there. I'm going to have to teach her a thing or two about escaping.

I guess she didn't know I killed those three last night. She was sleeping, but I would've told her when she got up, because we'd need to be moving on. I can't blame her for that. Still, I've been nothing but polite, and she runs off anyway. Maybe I should have changed my shirt earlier.

Calming down is harder than anticipated, and I need to be calm to figure out where she might've gone. If I'm fuming about her betrayal, I might miss something. I can be angry later. Deep breaths, counting to five on the in and out over and over until I feel my blood drop to a more normal temperature. She couldn't've gotten far.

The deep breaths bring in the scents of the morning forest. Moss, dirt, sunshine. The smell of dew evaporating, and the crispness of leaves starting to turn. Even though I'm not much of a woodsman, I can still appreciate the calm beauty here. Yet, I want to hammer my fists into the nearest tree, bark spraying everywhere, until it falls over.

Get over it. I'll get her back. Maybe she's confused, but more likely she's stubborn. From the very first, when she began her investigation two years ago, she's been tenacious and bull-headed. No reason she'd stop being that way now. I allow a small chuckle as I climb into the SUV. Zero's kept me on my toes, at least. Never a dull moment. I shouldn't have fallen asleep.

I back up the SUV and make a one-eighty. Tapping the gas to get going, but not too fast in case she made it fifteen feet and broke her ankle, I bump down the dirt road.

The first turn is right ahead. Too late I notice the dark bulk on the other side of the trees, focused as I am on scanning the woods to the left. I hit the brakes, hands gripping the steering wheel as the car darts forward and clips my front bumper, canting me and the SUV over into an odd angle.

I don't need to process to know exactly what happened and what's going on. Costecu sent more than one group. They found the ones I pitched over the side of the road, or they were already on their way. I was too slow in getting out, too complacent. I underestimated Costecu, and now they're here and I'm in big trouble.

Dazed, but not letting it bother me, I throw open my door and drop to the ground as gunfire rings out. Pops and shatters break the morning peace as the SUV bears the brunt of the assault. I crawl around toward the back as the window sprays glass on me from above. Costecu doesn't usually let his minions have guns, which means I'm fucked. He's serious about this, and they're likely to shoot me in a rush of newfound power.

On my stomach, elbows digging in the dirt as I scoot forward, I peek around the back as the firing slows and then stops. I see two, but I'd be willing to bet there's more.

"Come on out, Drew," one shouts, my name an epithet on his tongue. "We've got your girlfriend. Give up and I won't blow her head off."

I blink, confused for a full second trying to figure out who he's talking about. The answer hits me as he opens the door and drags Zero out of the back seat of the car. Shit. She's got a black eye but looks okay otherwise. I can tell because she's glaring at the guy with pure poison, even with his gun pointed in her direction. I'm worried she might try something and get herself killed.

I don't want her dead.

"How do I know you won't anyway?" I shout back. No point in trying to pretend I'm not here, and maybe she won't try anything stupid while I'm around.

"I guess you don't."

"That's not filling me with confidence," I reply. I sneak another peek around the side to look at Zero again. Her face has morphed into something besides rage. It's confusion, brows drawn together, mouth open a tantalizing amount, eyes flickering toward my voice.

"Get out here or I'll fill her with lead."

Not particularly threatening, but now isn't the time to discuss his intimidation tactics. We can do it later as I'm pulling out his teeth for touching Zero.

"Okay, I'm going to stand up and walk out. I'm not armed." I stand, put my hands up, and step out from behind the SUV. Now I can see there's four of them, and they all have guns. When it was two, I was hoping to get close enough to take them out. Even in a four versus one I'd try it, but not with Zero right there. There's almost no chance she wouldn't get hurt. I'd be willing to risk a broken arm or leg for her, but there are too many weapons and too big a chance she'd get shot.

For once Zero isn't glaring at me, but everyone else is. All the weapons are trained on me, and for a moment I think it might all be over, but no more shots happen. Costecu must have told them not to do anything but capture me, which is good in the short term, but bad in the long term. They'll call him and he'll come here, and not by himself. I have a little time to figure out a plan.

"What are you going to do?" I ask, buying time. Maybe they'll tell me, too. That would be nice.

"None of your business," the presumed leader says as the other three move forward to grab me. He's got a bit of a brain on him. I don't remember his name, but I recognize him as a werewolf.

I allow myself to be wrestled and shoved back down the road toward my cabin. Big Brain walks behind with Zero making displeased noises as he pulls her with him.

"What the fuck is going on?" she demands. I can picture the scowl on her face.

"You're in big fucking trouble is what's going on," Big Brain Werewolf says.

"No shit. Why did you attack Lindberg? How did you find me? Is Costecu coming? Why—"

Her questions are cut off with a meaty sound, maybe an elbow to the stomach because she bursts into coughs. Now I'm going to pull out all his fingernails, too.

"Shut up, don't be stupid," he growls.

We're escorted up the steps and back inside the cabin.

"Nice place," the leader sneers before I'm pushed down onto the couch. He shoves Zero down next to me. "I'm gonna enjoy coming out here when you're dead."

"Make yourself at home. There's ice cream in the freezer."

"You two, make sure there's no surprises or anything," he says, ignoring me. He stands between us and the fireplace, gun still drawn. They move off to poke around my belongings.

"Please, sit," I say, biding time. "Are you sure you don't want the ice cream? I have pizza, too. You're not vegan, are you?"

"Shut up."

"Trying to be a good host." If he sat down I might be able to get the drop on him. He must've been listening to some of the training I've given out, because he doesn't move. I couldn't teach garbage all the time, or it would be too obvious. It's also possible he's not a complete idiot. I'll withhold judgment for now.

"Look what we found," one of the others says, coming out of the bathroom with Zero's panties. "You wanna tell us something, Lindberg?"

"Obviously not mine."

"Put those down," Zero grumbles. I look over to see her face turning red.

They haven't tied me up yet, which is a massive mistake. Maybe I can distract them enough so they won't try until it's too late.

"I mean, sure, I fucked her." I shrug, as if it's a casual thing. "She got so wet she tried to clean them in the sink."

They all burst into laughter. Zero doesn't say anything, but her anger doesn't need words. It's a physical entity sitting between us, hot and burning. If I looked at her, I wouldn't be surprised to see literal fire coming out of her eyes.

"No we fucking didn't," she doesn't shout.

"Aw, don't deny it, sweetie," I say, nudging her in the ribs with an elbow. "It's nothing to be embarrassed about."

"She spicy? She looks like she's a secret slut or something with that temper." Now all the men are gathered around, leering. The woman is behind them but still interested.

"Oh, hell yeah," I continue, warming up to the performance and keeping a close watch on them. "You would not believe the stuff she wanted me to do."

A low rumble indicating a volcano about to erupt emanates from Zero.

"Like what?"

They're way too interested in this and it's gross, but I need to goad them on. "Okay, you ready for this?" I lean in like I'm going to divulge the biggest secret ever. "She wanted me to put that cucumber up her pussy."

"Oh shit, I picked up that thing up."

"Whoa."

"I didn't, but that's what she wanted." I lean back again. What a bunch of teenagers. Zero has gone from furious to whatever's past furious. When we get out of this I'm going to have to teach her a sense of humor. "That's not all, though."

"Oh yeah?"

"Yeah, get this." I lean forward, elbows on my knees, and this time they all lean in a little as well. I shift weight to my feet as I talk. "When we were in the middle of fucking? Like, right in the middle of it, my dick buried in her pussy?" I pause, relishing this story I'm making up, and reeling them in further.

"Well? What?" one asks after a sufficient pause.

Casual as anything, I put my hands on my knees, allowing me to lean forward more and taking almost all my weight on the balls of my feet. "She wanted me to call her..."

The tension in the air is palpable.

"What, man?"

Smooth as silk, I rise up and barrel into all of them.

"Get away, Zero," I shout, driving my legs and powering forward. I push them all backwards, smacking into the woman behind the men a split-second later. None of them have their feet planted, and the element of surprise is on my side. We crash into the fireplace in a tumble of arms and legs, and shouting anger.

The first few seconds in any fight are the most important. Before your opponent can figure out your rhythm you have an opening to stun them, take them out of theirs, and get the upper hand. I swing out with my fists, elbows, and knees. Anything I connect with will be victory. It's not pretty, and you won't find any videos on how to fight like this on YouTube, but when it's four versus one any sort of rules are off the table. I never follow rules anyway.

One of my fists impacts on something soft with bone underneath. The other elbow plows into something much harder, and a crack I feel more than hear is accompanied by a howl. Any second one of them is going to remember they've got a gun and start firing.

Hands are grabbing and pushing at me, scrabbling and frantic. They're all shouting at each other and me, a chaotic mess of voices and animalistic sounds only serving to confuse things more. Something pierces my side. A hand is pushing at my face. I bite it.

I'm pushed back, and someone rises up to my left. Using my head like a wrecking ball I put them down while trying to find a weapon in the mess of muscles and clothing. The pain in my side is sharp, but ignorable for now. Vision blurred by adrenaline, nostrils overwhelmed by the onslaught of sweat and fear, and piss.

Vision goes bright, pain in my right ear. My hands are too busy searching to defend myself. Twisting and clawing. Something hard and cold, metal, I've got the barrel. Someone has the trigger, a shot rings out, muffled by bodies. A cry. No time to decide if it's me, grabbing at the hand, squeezing and crushing. I'm pushed back again, hanging on to the gun and the hand. There's a slither to the left, I get a foot under me to stop my backward movement.

I hope Zero got away.

Another shot, this one louder, no longer muzzled. A noise like a boulder breaking rips my eardrums, and stinging crackles in my leg. Not the gun I'm holding since the fingers under my hand are pulverized into jelly. I wrench. Someone screams.

I'm on one knee, the four targets all in front of me. Finger squeezing, the recoil compensated for by muscle memory. Even with blurred sight it's hard to miss at this range, I fire twice at each. They drop, all in less than three seconds, writhing on the ground. Silver bullets, of course. Even if you aren't a werewolf or vampire they'll still hurt.

I pause to catch a breath, then stand up to finish it. Two bullets in each head. I have to stoop to pick up another discarded pistol after finishing off the second body because the magazine is empty. One of them pleads and cries. I hate cowardice.

Blood oozes everywhere. It's going to soak into the floor and stain it forever, and the area rug is ruined. One twitches and I fire again to be sure. Half the head is missing, but some creatures are persistent.

The silence is profound, even through the ringing of my ears. After something intense the silence is always deep, as if all the birds and insects around have stopped out of respect or fear.

I'm holding my side. Some of my own blood is seeping from between my fingers. That damn werewolf sunk his claws into me.

"Fucking shit," someone says.

I spin, tense again, alert, but it's only Zero. She's standing there with the iron fireplace poker cocked behind her head like she's about to swing at a baseball. Her eyes are enormous, fixed on the mess on the floor.

I toss my used pistol on the chair and pluck the improvised weapon from her hands. She doesn't move.

"Oh fuck," she repeats.

"I'm sure you've seen dead bodies," I say, pushing her arms down because she doesn't seem capable of doing it herself. "You were there when you caught me, remember?"

"I—not up—not while…"

Grabbing her hips, I guide her backward, and then settle her butt down onto the cushions, blocking her view of most of it. "Not so up close and personal?"

Her eyes glide to my side. "You're bleeding."

"Yup. It happens."

"Uh, I, uh—fuck."

Shit. She's in shock. I should've known. Maybe she's been in the field a few times, and handled some interrogations, but seeing a few dead bodies isn't the same as seeing them go from alive to dead, and all the gore that goes with it.

"Come on, let's get you out of the room." I go to scoop her up, but she jerks back and pushes at my arms.

"No, I'm—it's fine. I'm fine, it's okay."

"Zero, you're in shock."

"No shit. It's fine. I'm not a god damned—it's fine."

"It's not fine," I protest, reaching for her again.

Again, she pushes away my hands. "Tell me how I can help." Her gaze connects with mine. There's something there, a diamond at the center of those emeralds. Determination.

Never have I ever been so attracted to someone. The hints were always there, but this moment, standing in front of a pile of bodies, is a moment I'll always remember. The moment she refused to give in for even one second.

In this moment, she's captured me forever.

CHAPTER TWENTY-ONE

Aideen

My brain is having a hard time comprehending everything around me, so I focus on one bite-sized chunk at a time.

Lindberg is really trying to save me, not setting an elaborate trap. It was obvious, of course, but I didn't want to believe it. Now I have no choice. Not with four dead people bleeding all over his fireplace. I dance away from that fact for now.

Blood is coming from his side at an alarming rate, and I'm pretty sure he was shot in the leg, too. His ear is bleeding. Based on the rate his hand is swelling, it's probably broken. His clothes are ruined. He left a bloody handprint on his pants I'm wearing.

"Do you have a first-aid kit?" I ask. I can bandage his wounds. I'll worry about the bodies later. They aren't going anywhere.

"Kitchen sink," Lindberg says. A touch of a slur mars his deep voice as he drops into the other chair. The blood loss can't be good.

I'm up and off the couch, wanting to run into the kitchen and tear through the cabinets to find the kit, but I stay calm. There's no reason to rush and panicking might cause him to panic, too. He probably panics every day. The only reason I'm panicking is because I don't want him to die.

The kit is under the sink, like he said, neatly to the side against the cabinet wall. I've never seen such a clean under-the-sink cabinet. It doesn't look like any water has ever touched any of the surfaces. If I had more time, I'd admire it further, but I need to try to fix him up.

Back around the cabinets and into the living room, it's easier to avoid looking at the dead bodies. Lindberg is leaning back, his head tipped over the top of the chair, his eyes closed. He's still gripping his side, and blood is still flowing. It's thicker and slower than blood flow I've seen before.

"How do you feel?" What a stupid question. Of course he feels awful.

"I'm fine."

"Don't try to be macho and stoic. Take off your shirt, I need to look at it."

The impact of my words hits me when he lifts his head and stares at me.

"It'll be fine," he repeats, but starts to unbutton his shirt anyway.

Okay. So he's going to take off his shirt. His chest appears in an ever-widening triangle as his big fingers pop each button out of its slot. A splash of hair dusts across his pecs and down the middle of his muscular abs. The trail goes all the way down, over and past his navel, and a thrill wracks my knees to see it disappear into the top of his pants. Our tenuous connection is turning my tongue into rubber. He pulls the shirt all the way open to shrug out of it.

It's okay for me to stare at his chest. I have to stare because I have to look at his wound. One hundred percent normal to trace the hard ridges and dips with my gaze and wonder what it would feel like to trace them with my tongue.

"You okay, Zero?"

I avoid looking into his eyes, because I'm afraid he's going to see how turned on I am, but they burn into my forehead as if he can read my thoughts. I'm reminded of all those days ago, which feel like years, when I felt the same intense stare through the security glass. My thoughts now are even dirtier than back then. "Of course," I reply, voice as steady as Jell-O.

Before meeting Drew, I'd never blushed this often, and I try not to now, no matter how hot my blood is thrumming in my veins. It's a reaction to the situation, nothing more. Adrenaline coming down or something. There's nothing going on, no basis for this desire I can't stop feeling.

He winces as he rolls his shoulder to try to get the shirt off. I lurch forward to help, knocked out of my trance once his gaze drops from my face. Moving behind him helps ease the pressure in my head and pesky other places, until I touch his shoulders to pull the shirt back.

I had no idea the sight of flexing muscles, each one defined in perfect clarity, was such a turn-on. I've never dated anyone like Lindberg. I always went for the intelligent, soft-spoken, polite types. The guys who would be comfortable discussing 18th century Russian politics, or the history of opera while sipping a coffee they ground themselves. Working out was a thing they did with reluctance, and only enough to stave off the ravages of time a bit longer.

Yet, here is this man, this enormous man with muscles I wouldn't be surprised to discover have their own muscles. He's not polite, not in the deferring way most people are, and the way he stares at me leaves no questions about what he wants to do.

Maybe that's what's got me so out of sorts. Other guys would dance around, gauge my interest, pretend to like what I like. Lindberg would just grab and take me, like he grabbed and took the life of the four people still laying in a grotesque tangle behind me.

So why hasn't he? Three aching points are demanding to be taken. Taken by him, and his fingers, his mouth, and his—

"What are you doing, Zero?" he asks, an edge of rasp to his voice.

My hands are still on his shoulders, fingers pressing the hardness, while I swim in hormones.

"Helping," I manage, even though I'm the one needing help. I pull at the fabric.

He has a tattoo on the back of his left shoulder. It's some sort of jagged and linear script, something I recognize as letters, but not in English or Russian.

He grunts, either in reply or in pain, I can't tell. Together we manage to get the ruined and expensive shirt off. He pulls himself up into a better position and twists to look down at where his side was pierced by the claws. So many muscles do their muscle-y thing.

Thick blood is smeared all over the wound, and I almost lose my breakfast of chips and water. It's not the blood itself getting to me, it's the thought of *his* blood oozing everywhere. He's not supposed to bleed. He's supposed to be invulnerable.

Forcing myself to ignore that dangerous line of thought, I move around the chair, pick up the kit, and open it up. Gauze, scissors, thread and needle, all the usual stuff is in there.

"We need to clean it," I say, because I need to say something. I need to focus on this task, and not anything else. I put on the nitrile gloves and grab the wipes. "This is going to hurt, probably."

He flinches a little as I wipe away the mess, which causes my temperature to rise. It's a reminder he's a real person, a real person with real needs. Needs I can guess at every time I look into his eyes.

"How is it so thick?" I ask about the blood to try to distract myself. It doesn't work because my lust-addled brain supplies another part of him I could use that line on.

"Ever hear the phrase 'blood from a stone?' Dwarves don't bleed so much."

If this isn't so much, then I shudder to think what real damage would look like. I keep at it, until half the pack of wipes later it's as clean as I can get it. The holes aren't deep or long, only a few inches.

"You got lucky." I use an excuse to explore his body with my fingers, being careful not to hurt him, not able to ignore who I'm touching. His skin is hot, taut, and even with the rips through it I can't help but notice how I don't want to stop touching it.

"Nope. Takes more than some idiotic werewolf to put me down. Maybe I can't heal in the shower, but you're forgetting your lore."

I glance up. "I didn't think you peeked." Before I can decide how turned on I feel about him looking at me while I showered, he replies.

"I didn't." His look is reproachful, as if I hurt his feelings. "But you seem to be using those fingers without a problem, and you haven't limped at all."

"Oh. Yeah." I'm so out of sorts I can't even think logically for five seconds. It's also obvious why he's not too hurt. Dwarves aren't only dense in the head, they're dense everywhere. Their bones are heavy, and it takes some work to pierce their skin. If it had been me, I'm sure I'd have been ripped in half.

Needing to ignore the thoughts of ripping and shredding, I thread the special needle in preparation to stitch him up.

As I'm laying my hand on him, repressing the shaking in my hand, he grabs my wrist.

"Hey, wha—"

"Shut up," he growls, staring at the door.

I open my mouth to protest again, but his glare fixes on me for a half-second, and I've never been so scared. They're dark, hard, and warn me if I say anything he's going to get angry in a way I've never seen. I shut my gaping mouth.

For long seconds with my wrist captured in his hand as securely as a key in a lock, I don't breathe or move. Waiting, I hear nothing, smell nothing, and see nothing out of the ordinary. He must be sensing something with heightened abilities I don't have. Right before it gets to the point where I'm memorizing how it feels to have his fingers pressing down on my pulse, he stands, dragging me up with him.

"Go hide, Zero."

"What? Why?"

He looks at me again, and this time it's not in anger. It's intense in a different way. "Because running won't help you, but I don't want you to see this."

"See what?"

"For fuck's sake, Zero, are you going to question everything I tell you?" For a brief moment it looks like he wants to laugh, but then the lines on his face settle back down into dead seriousness. Dropping my wrist, he reaches around to place his hand around the base of my neck, spins me around, and taps his palm between my shoulders. It's a move with connotations unthought about until this moment. "Hide. Now."

"If I can't run, hiding isn't going to work either," I say spinning back around.

"Jesus fuck," he mutters. "You're so stubborn. I don't have time for this."

With quickness that would be surprising if I hadn't seen it already, he grabs me and I'm tossed over his shoulder. A few long strides and we're in the bedroom. He tosses me, full body, onto the bed from the door. I bounce hard and trying my best to ignore the thrill running through me. Before I can do more than scramble off the mattress, he's slammed the door shut with a click.

"Are you serious?" I shout through the wood, pounding my fists on it. "You can't lock me up in here."

If he's still out there he doesn't answer. I throw myself on the bed, grab at the bottom of the window and tug. It doesn't move. I try harder, muscles straining. Checking for a lock or latch, and finding none, I attack the window again, furious and frantic. I can't articulate why I need to get out of here, but I do.

I want to get out of here and attack Lindberg, make him pay for all his little gestures of disrespect and condescension. Not once has he allowed me to make my own decisions. I don't know what's about to happen, even though I sense it's something bad, and I want to help. Instead, I'm locked up in this stupid bedroom, shouting and pounding the glass, running over to the door to pound and yank on the doorknob. Nothing helps, and I get no response.

A horrible screech rends the air, shattering my anger, freezing me in my tracks. It's like nothing I've ever heard before, simultaneously rumbling in my bones and scratching across my eardrums. Every uncomfortable sensation associated with sound flays across my skin and mind, and I stagger back from the door, clamping my hands over my ears. It doesn't help.

The sound stops as soon as it starts, although even those few moments were enough for me to not want to hear it again. I flop down onto the bed, exhausted from the effort of being subjected to the noise. The silence afterwards is as loud as the scream, until another shout sounds out. This one is not as horrifying to my ears, but it still sends a chill down my spine. That was Lindberg. He sounded like a monster from the core of the earth.

I scrabble on my hands and knees across the sheets to the window again, pressing my face to the glass. I look left and right, up and even down, trying to see anything, but this room is at the back of the cabin, opposite from the noises.

Another terrible scream, although this one is not as loud, and almost bearable. It still scratches across my teeth. With nothing else to do I fling myself at the door again, ramming my shoulder into it. The only thing I get is a bruised shoulder and more frustration.

The sounds are mingling now, a ferocious cacophony of anger.

Think, woman, think. Use your brain, not your brawn. The room is only a room. A typical bedroom I'd slept in. Lamp, picture frames, dresser with clothes. Bed, mattress, window, door. Without any better idea I fling open the dresser doors, slamming Lindberg's shirts and slacks back and forth on their hangers.

With nothing there, I dash to one of the bedside tables and yank the drawer, pulling it open. There are grooming tools, a nail file and scissors, comb, brush. The second water bottle is still in the oversized pockets of his pants I'm wearing.

I pull it out, mind racing, twist the top off, and pour the water onto the floor. Impatient while it glugs like molasses in winter, I grab the tiny scissors and stab the plastic, twisting and making a hole. Air rushes in, and the rest of the water glugs out. I cut, fingers hurting as the small metal grips dig in with every squeeze. After what seems like a million years I've finally cut a rectangle of plastic out of the bottle.

Running back to the door, avoiding the water puddle I've left, I shove the plastic into the jamb above the deadbolt. Jigging, pushing, twisting, and cursing, I work the knob and with a satisfying feeling of metal sliding back, the door pops open.

Throwing it open, running out as fast as I can manage with the cuffs of the pants now dangerously close to tripping me, I barrel past the bodies, unseeing, and open the front door.

I only have a split second to register what's going on, but it turns my blood cold. Lindberg is on the ground, pinned by some creature at least twice his size. The creature who must've made those horrible sounds. Talons on the front legs are pricking at Lindberg's bare chest, a head like a snake looming over his face. The similarity to a snake doesn't end there, as the front half of it is covered in scales, which turn into feathers halfway down the body. Back legs are feathered too, with even crueler talons unsheathed. The tail is long, plumed, and twitching from side to side like a cat.

I don't realize I've made any noise, until they both turn to look at me. I recognize the face. It's Gil. Gil the dragon, and he's about five seconds from killing Lindberg.

"Zero," Lindberg shouts. "Fucking run."

Something inside snaps. I'm tired of being threatened, beat up, and ordered around. Lindberg treats me like I couldn't take care of myself, but that couldn't be further from the truth. I can defend myself if I have to. I'm successful and independent, and I don't need him and his grasping hands and searing gaze.

If this dragon thinks he's going to take that away from me without a fight, he's wrong.

Sparing only a half-second wishing I had my talisman so I'd be at full strength, I launch myself off the porch and land with a thump on Gil's scaled back. Before either of them can react, I bite down as near to the base of the neck as I can figure.

It's been a while since I've bitten anyone for real. Disused jaw muscles strain against the scales plating Gil's back, until with a satisfying crunch I break through. His weird scream lights up my ears at the same time as the hot taste of blood spurts into my mouth.

Shaking my head a little to tear a bit more then releasing, I spit out the horrible taste in my mouth as he rises up on his back legs in an attempt to buck me off. Clinging tight while Lindberg shouts something down below, I'm confronted with the snarling face of Gil at the end of his neck.

He snaps at me, cat-like. I flinch back, losing my grip, and slide down his back. With a flick of his tail, I'm flung against the wall of the cabin, crashing into solid wood.

"Zero," Lindberg yells again, echoing through my ears as everything goes black.

CHAPTER TWENTY-TWO

Druain

Zero goes down like a sack of stones, Gil's tail snagging her legs and pulling hard.

"Zero," I shout, as if my voice can cushion her from the fall. All I wanted her to do was stay out of sight, get a few more minutes of life in peace. I didn't have a good plan. Maybe bargain for her life in some way, although I have nothing to give Gil he couldn't take. He doesn't want money or anything material. The only thing I have to give him is myself as food, and he's about to take that anyway.

There aren't any other options. If she runs, he'll track her down in minutes, and then she'll die scared in the woods, rather than scared in the comfort of a cabin. I'd thought about snapping her neck and ending it quick and painless, but I couldn't bring myself to do it. There's always the possibility she can figure some way out, and I won't deny her the chance, even if it means there's a greater chance of going out in terror.

I'm a coward.

Now she's stunned, laid out on the deck, Gil's tail wrapped around her and his gaze fixed on her prone body. He's going to kill her, and I let it happen by not acting quickly enough. I allowed myself to get complacent, believing in the security I thought I provided. Instead, I've been lazy and careless, basking in overconfidence. I'm not only a coward, I'm stupid.

Everything has been a waste. All my work for nothing. All those people, all this time, everything I've sacrificed, for nothing. Everything Zero has done, for nothing. Ended on the talons of a stupid, scaly, savage dragon.

Her arm is flung out in front of her, but over it I can see the top of her head, one of her eyes. Closed, as if in sleep, hair a tangled mess. Still in my clothes. A shirt far too big hiding her figure, pants only staying on with help from the belt she's twisted around her waist.

No. No, I won't let it happen, I won't let us end. I won't let her end. Anger surges through me, a white-hot rush of iron in my veins, heating me from the inside out, lighting every nerve and muscle. I'm still alive, and I'll fight every moment to keep it that way.

All this in half a second, a sliver of time while Gil has turned to look at his fallen prey.

I grab a talon in each fist, and with a shout I don't recognize, wrench up as hard as possible. It's nowhere near as easy as when I'd done the same to Zero, but the satisfying crunch as bone and tendons snap fills my ears.

He screams, or screeches, a sound which pierces like needles in my ears and pounds like drums in my chest. His head whips back around, changing his focus from Zero. I punch him in whatever he has for a nose, then again and again, vision going dark in fury.

The talons on his other foot dig into my chest, puncturing skin all along my rib cage. Grabbing his serpentine face, I extend my fingers to search for his eyes, something soft to injure. He screams again as I find my targets. I'm glad I haven't eaten anything today, because the way those sounds make my stomach quiver, I might have lost it.

The tactic works. The weight on my chest shifts as he moves to grab at my arms. Talons pierce there, but I'd rather lose a hand than my chest. I surge up, slamming my forehead into the blunt point of his snout. I misjudge and end up smashing into his teeth. They scrape across my forehead, but I feel a couple of cracks.

Carrying my momentum forward as much as I can, I get my foot under me, bracing against him as he tries to crush me down. He's bigger, but four legs are harder and slower than two. A twist and a roll and I'm beside him. The loss of force pushing against him is sudden, and he falls to the ground on all fours.

I punch him in the side of the head.

He only got me the first time because I wasn't focused. I was thinking too much about how he'd got here, and who else was lurking. Those angry yells trailing after me when I locked Zero in her room.

I'd run out the door and been blindsided. Gil had been waiting on the roof and pounced on me the instant I was off the deck. The resulting struggle had been one-sided, and only Zero showing up, something I should've expected, saved me.

I punch him again as he twists his head on his long neck to try to bite me. His tail lashes out from the other direction, but I grab it and hold on tight. He tries to turn, four legs scrabbling in the dirt, so I follow, staying next to his side. Any time he tries to bite I hit him.

Talons from the back leg grabs me around my leg while he swipes from the front. He tries to pull me down from the back. Warmth seeps down my calf. Blood. I resist the urge to kick back, which would only cause more tearing, and keep focusing on pounding my free fist into the side of his face.

Sound is muddled, full of grunts, bone on bone, and trampling in the grass. If I can stay close to him, I'll have the advantage, and he knows it, trying to get me away, out of the range of my fists and into the range of his talons and tail.

His tail is still wrapped in my fist, and he yanks at the same time as his grip tightens on my leg. I stumble, unable to muscle through the sudden tug. He cries out in triumph, pulls harder, and manages to fling me backwards. I trip over the steps and tumble down.

Gil turns, free of my hold, and now the only thing in front of me is his face and front claws, neither of which I want to attack directly.

His muscles bunch along his back legs, a pause before he leaps, giving me a fraction of a second to roll, avoiding the deadly attack. The wood of the deck transitions to the hard ground as I bump over the steps and fall, rolling more and trying to get up, expecting him to grab me again with those wicked talons.

I get far enough away and bounce up into a crouch and then to my feet. Gil is in front of me, grabbing, and I have to drop and roll again, this time behind him. He growls and tries to follow. I jump on his back and hold on tight as he tries to buck me off.

This isn't an ideal situation, but nothing about fighting Gil is ideal. I hope Zero doesn't wake up now to see how stupid I look, holding on like some yuppie on a mechanical bull, trying to impress his girlfriend.

I sort of wish Gil had wings so I'd have something to hold on to. He swings his head around to snap at me, so I grab it instead.

Because I have to win this before he tires me out, I take a risk and punch into his mouth, fist impacting into his throat. He gags, flinging his head to the side and scraping my arm with his teeth. I notice the ones I'd broken with some satisfaction, but there's no time to dwell on past accomplishments.

Taking the opening while he's dazed, I grab his lower jaw in both hands, make a small leap, and fall to the ground. My weight wrenches his head down, and if it hadn't been for his long neck, his jaw would have snapped off. As it is, I still get his head twisted down and around. I'm between his front feet, staring into his upside-down head.

Scrabbling back and pulling, even as he clamps his mouth shut and all my fingers are trapped between sharp razors, I yank hard, moving under him, pulling his jaw and neck, twisting. His feet do a dance as he tries to figure out which way to go, while a high-pitched whine streams from his throat. He gets one foot over, stepping on me, but he's unbalanced, and with a shoulder shove the foot kicks back out. Still pulling on his jaw, I push up to my feet, ramming my back into his underbelly. Together we lurch up, and then, slow as an ancient oak, we topple over sideways. I feel the air rush from his lungs as I ram into him, and his mouth pops open with the force.

Getting my foot under me, I plant the other on his stomach while his legs flail for purchase. He doesn't remind me of a cat now. He reminds me of a cow who's fallen over. Twisting hard, even as his jaw closes over my fingers, I feel it start to break. He struggles harder, moving me back in the grass, his muscles straining against my foot, but then with a final bit of resistance, the jaw tears away. A crack like a gunshot, a squeal from the world's biggest pig, and I've got it in my hands, stringy flesh dangling from the ripped edges.

Blood blooms instantly along those edges, and Gil no longer scrambles with purpose, but is writhing in pain. I throw the jaw aside, and move to run up the steps. Zero is sitting up, looking horrified, mouth open and hands halfway to her face.

"Get me a gun," I shout.

She doesn't move, her stare fixed on Gil. I leap past her into the cabin, no time to snap her out of it, grab one of the pistols from the other attackers, and dash back outside. Gil is trying to crawl up the steps, heaving his body toward Zero who is trying to scrabble away, trapped by the corner of the porch.

He's mad now, and if I left him like this he'd probably be okay, although he'd be eating with a straw from now on. I'm not going to leave him like this.

Stepping in front of her, shoving Zero back further with my foot, I grab him, jam the gun against the soft part in the roof of his mouth and fire until the clip is empty.

Each loud shot is accompanied by one of those wrenching screams, until I get to the final couple. He won't be pissed off—or anything else—anymore.

There's nothing left of the top of his head, just a bloody mess leaking all over my hand. I let the corpse go, and it flops to the deck, about five feet from where Zero is still crouched behind me.

I don't turn to look at her yet. We're either safe, or very fucked. If Costecu is around, sending people in waves to get me, then there's no way he won't appear within a couple of minutes. If no one else comes, then I can relax for a short period of time.

My hands and arms are covered in blood, both mine and Gil's. My leg is on fire from the injury. Sweat stings my eyes and coats my chest in a thin sheen. I don't ache yet, but I will.

Zero's breathing is loud and ragged, although she hasn't screamed and she isn't whimpering. All the birds have fled. No other sounds break the silence in the aftermath.

"I guess I win the pool," I say after another minute of silence. "I wonder if they'll let me collect."

Zero bursts into a series of uncontrolled giggles while staring at Gil's sprawled bulk. Alarm bells go off in my head. A noise like that shouldn't leave her lips. It's wrong. Zero laughs. She doesn't giggle like a little girl.

"Let's get you inside," I say, tossing the gun away and reaching down a stained hand.

She doesn't react.

"Zero. Let's go. Inside."

Something in my voice must catch her attention, because she looks up, eyes unblinking. "You're bloody."

Vexing woman. With an exasperated sigh I reach down and grab her upper arm, smearing drying blood across the fabric of my shirt she's tucked into. She doesn't resist as I pull her upright, and with my hand on her back, I maneuver her to the door. I have to open it myself to nudge her inside.

She stops as soon as we cross the threshold, staring at the dead people, her whole body tensing to the point of rigidity. All this might have been too much. Being as careful as possible, I grab her around the waist, lift her over the back of the couch, and set her down.

A quick journey into the kitchen, and I bring back a bottle of water and the other bag of chips and drop those next to her. "Eat. Drink."

My next goal is clearing the bodies from her sight. She doesn't move as I grab each corpse under their shoulders and drag them out, tossing them in a pile at the side of the cabin. At no point does she go for the chips or water. Gil is harder to drag, but after a twenty-minute struggle, he ends up with the rest of the corpses. A compost heap of horrors. I'm going to have to burn them, and it's going to stink.

Back inside, Zero is still sitting on the couch, staring at the vacant patch on the floor that's covered in blood. Maybe a quick change of view will help. Picking her up again, I carry her to her bedroom, almost slip on a mysterious puddle of water, and then go back for her food and drink. I rip open the bag of chips and drop it in her lap. She doesn't move, still staring, but at nothing but wall.

"Zero." I snap my fingers in front of her face.

She flinches back, eyes rooted to my hand. "Bloody."

I growl, spin, and stomp to the bathroom. Stripping off my pants, turning on the water, I step into the shower without waiting for it to warm up. I wash. The soap stings my wounds, but the water washes it all away, and turns from red to brown to clear in a matter of minutes. I'll have a new scar or two, but most of what happened won't be lasting.

Out of the shower, the lone towel does a good enough job of drying. I wrap it around my waist, snug it tight, and head back to Zero. Her hand is in the chip bag.

"Better?"

She looks up from the floor, a pause as her gaze run over me. "You showered."

"Yeah."

There's another pause. She crunches a chip. "Then can you tell me what the fuck is going on?"

Her tone is challenging, almost angry. I stare at her in disbelief. "I just fucking killed like five people to keep you safe, is what's going on."

She shoots up, the bag falling to the floor, barbeque chips spilling across the wood. The shirt slides down when she stabs a finger in my direction, revealing one bare shoulder. "You call this safe?"

"Do you see anyone trying to kill you?" I look around, arms spread.

"Are you fucking kidding me?" she shouts. Her face flushes, lips curled in anger. "Since I met you there's been nothing *but* people trying to kill me. Everyone around you is a killer, and I'm only alive 'cause you've been the better killer."

"I'm fucking sorry for helping," I shout back, stepping into her space and looking down into her snapping eyes. "Maybe I should have tried to talk to them. I'm sure they would've changed their minds."

"Maybe you should think about what you're doing for once." She doesn't back down, planting her bare hand on my chest and trying to shove.

My heart is pounding in anger. Her hand feels like fire on my skin. "I'm sorry I can't fucking think as good as you, but I am trying to protect you." I grab her bicep as she tries to push me.

"Don't be a condescending asshole, you fucker. I can protect myself," she shouts, pounding the side of her fist against me.

The utter gall to challenge me about my actions is extraordinary. "Because you were doing such a good job by yourself." I capture her other wrist to stop her from hitting me, even though it would be kind of fun in a different situation. She struggles against my grip, but I don't let go.

"I got all the way out here without your so-called help." She kicks me in the shin.

Fed up with this argument, and not having a third hand to grab her leg, I trip her and drive her down to the bed, arms above her head. Her hair splays behind her and her eyes shoot open in shock. Before she can protest further I smash my body down and crash my lips against hers.

I need this passionate woman right now more than anyone I've ever needed before.

CHAPTER TWENTY-THREE

Aideen

My temper is swirling around, a hurricane carrying the ship of adrenaline and emotions toward looming cliffs. Even though I want to turn around, pull everything back, I can't. The words spring from me, uncontrolled and wild. None of them are untrue, but I wish I could say them in a way that's less harsh. I have no desire to make Lindberg angry, but he needs to listen, and the only thing he seems to listen to is strength.

I'm tired of being shoved around, put in places of danger over and over. His excuse he's trying to protect me burns like a brand, searing my consciousness. It's only an excuse, he doesn't mean it, it's a way to justify how he's treated me. Slapping, picking up and throwing, dragging me around like a toy on leash. Any time I've been with him he's never let me be more than five feet from him.

Then there was the fight with what must have been Gil. A real dragon. Cruel and ugly, a being who could never go out in public. The only life he's known has doubtless been the dark world of Costecu's underground, wherever it might have been at the time. I almost felt sorry for him.

I'd gained consciousness in time to watch the end of the fight, looking away when it was clear Lindberg was going to pull off Gil's jaw. That level of violence is not something I'm comfortable with. Part of the reason I'm reacting so strongly is because I'm ashamed I broke down as far as I did. Showing such weakness in front of Lindberg made me feel worthless, which is another emotion I don't care to explore, and I took it out on him.

The only response I have is denial and physical violence, but of course I'm no match for him. He grabs me, pushes me, and finally kicks my legs out from under me. The wind is knocked out of my lungs, and not by the fall, as I find myself tossed to the bed, Lindberg looming over me. His eyes are dark and crackling with magma, twin volcanoes ready to erupt.

His hands are huge and strong as they trap my wrists, and for the first time ever I feel one hundred percent small and helpless. I believe there was always a chance I'd be able to get away from any of the other situations, but not this time. Not that I want to get away. The thought sneaks in and sits up, but I'm not surprised. I can't even remember how long I've been fighting the urge.

As I'm about to give in and do what I want, which is lift my head and kiss him, he beats me to it. His lips find mine in a rush, hard and urgent, hard enough our teeth clack and a jolt of lightning spears my thoughts, pinning them in place. I can't think, only feel, as he takes my lips as if they're the sweetest chocolate.

I don't read romance novels. The cliches are rife, and the situations ridiculous, but I'll be damned if I don't feel a clench from what would be called my "core." More than a clench. If I'm being honest, it's a veritable earthquake down there. It gets stronger the longer the kiss goes on, which distracts me from the need to breathe.

The kiss ends when he wants it to. He releases me, not without dragging his teeth over my bottom lip, only to plant his mouth under the curve of my jaw. I can't do anything but tilt my head back, asking for more, as his lips and teeth conquer the skin on my neck.

His hand lands on my bare shoulder, slipped free of the shirt, and only then do I notice he's got both of my wrists in one hand. Somehow, through the scrambled mess of my brain, I get a signal out to tug at his grip, a small test. There's no give, and he rumbles some sort of low note against me. Goosebumps appear across the back of my neck.

I should be trying to stop him. This isn't right, it's unprofessional, and I hate his guts. All of those reasons seem logical enough, but it's drowned out by my stupid primal brain, begging for more, for everything. It's awash in lust, and there's nothing I can do to stop it.

The heat of his body is overwhelming mine, and I miss it when he pulls back, lifting up by pushing my hands down further into the mattress. For a moment, it looks as if he's going to say something—what, I can't fathom—but then his gaze meets mine.

I'm sure he can read my mind, to see what I want. The words I'm not able to speak must shine in my eyes, a signal of some sort he picks up on. Maybe it's my panting, or maybe it's the low moan I let escape my lips, but whatever it is, his hard hand on my shoulder is grabbing the collar of the shirt and yanking, hard.

The opposite side of the collar digs into my neck, but that's not what I notice. What I notice is all the buttons flying off in a shower of pops, a machine gun running down my chest. Cool air cascades over my skin, raising even more goosebumps, and then his gaze follows, drinking in my exposed breasts.

If I thought my nipples were hard a moment ago, it's nothing compared to what they feel like now. Tense, almost painful, the ache from them radiating into my heart, begging to be touched. He doesn't touch, or rub the pad of his thumb across them as others have done in the past. He grabs, hard, mauling me like a bear would a deer.

With a gasp of shock, my body arches up against his hand, driving my nipple deeper against his palm. His fingers squeeze harder around my mound, mirroring my gripping the sheets for dear life.

This is only heavy petting, or groping, and already it feels like I'm going to explode. The ache in my breasts is rivaled by the ache in my core—fuck it, my pussy. I open my mouth to say something, anything, to plead or beg, but before I can get any words out he's kissing me again. Another clench down below, and this time the moan I make is swallowed by his mouth.

His rough hand leaves my breast and glides down my chest, my waist, and then his fingers press into my skin as he tries to work it under the band of the pants. The belt is too tight, though, and for the first time he says something, lips moving against my own.

"God damn it, Zero."

I bite his lips, not holding back as he tries to fumble with the belt buckle one-handed. "Having trouble down there?" That I'm able to get words out is a wonder, much less sound so casual about it. Like I'm used to being manhandled by a seven-foot beast.

I'm rewarded with a growl and being dragged further onto the bed by my wrists. My hair, spread out around me, ends up caught underneath, tugging at my scalp and dragging a yelp from my throat, but he doesn't notice, or doesn't care. He's too focused on scrabbling with the now more accessible belt, thick fingers struggling with the knot I made to keep it on.

I'm about to egg him on with another quip, dying to see what he'd do, when the belt comes undone in a rush. It flaps away in the air like a bat, crashing against the wall, and then the cloth of the pants drags against my thighs as he yanks them down as far as they'll go. With no fanfare his thumb lands on my clit, a hawk swooping down on its prey.

"Fuck," I shout or moan, brain dissolving into mush. I can't do anything but roll my hips reaching for his whole hand. No other part of my body responds to any of the orders I give, but desire to do anything else melts away when the thumb journeys lower.

Don't get me wrong, he's not gentle, but I'd expected something rougher. Instead, the feeling of his thumb sliding into me is almost reverential, a slow slide parting my lips and pinning me in place.

"Fuck," he growls a few times against my neck, until his thumb is buried in me as deep as it can go and his palm is pressing down on my clit. "I've wanted this since the moment you walked into that room. All cocky and confident."

I babble something incoherent as he grinds his palm and curls his thumb up inside me, holding me in a vise-like grip of pleasure. All the tension coursing through my body has no outlet. My arms can't move, my legs are pinned under him, his teeth are claiming my neck, and he's got my pussy in a grip of steel.

"Don't hold back. Give me what I want."

To spite him, I try to do the exact opposite, but his thumb and palm are having none of it. Squeezing all my muscles in an attempt to contain the engine racing out of control only makes his thumb feel fuller. My tongue burns because I'm biting down on it as hard as I can.

"Zero," he says in my ear, his breath hot as lava. It's an invitation, but one I'm not allowed to refuse.

With a final squeeze from his fingers, my inner muscles clench up tight, harder than I've ever felt, almost painful. Then everything breaks, a spring past its limit, snapping with an audible noise bursting from my lips.

Everything goes dark, then colors flash across my vision as I regain my hearing only to listen to myself cry out like a wanton creature. If I had any sense of decorum I'd be embarrassed beyond words at the noises I'm making, but if that's the price to feel like this, then decorum can fuck off.

"Holy shit, Zero," Lindberg mutters above me. "How long has it been since someone's fucked you? I think you needed that."

"You haven't fucked me yet," I counter, panting and wanting more. "What are you waiting for?"

Through the haze I can see his eyebrows shoot up, and then before I have any time to react, I'm flipped over on my stomach and his pants are dragged off my legs all the way. His hand lands on my bare ass in a slap, the sudden sting from it a delightful contrast to the cool air sweeping over my heated skin.

"Be careful what you ask for," he says, and slaps me again. "You might get more than you can handle."

Twisting my head to lock my glare with his, I say what I hope will do the trick. "Is this you trying to intimidate me? I've handled everything you've thrown at me so far." My voice is less calm now, a slight tremor detectable to my own ears. How I can hear anything over the pounding of my heart is a miracle.

Another spank, harder than the last two, tears a squeak from my lungs. No one's ever spanked me before. I suspect because they were all afraid. Lindberg isn't afraid of anything.

Then his heavy palm lands square between my shoulders, smashing my upper body down into the mattress. He grabs the expensive cloth and pulls up hard, wrenching my arms back as the shirt is ripped from me. Before I can complain about how much it hurt, he's pinning me back down, rough skin scrubbing against the sensitive spot between my shoulder blades.

Drawing breath would be difficult with my lungs being smashed, but I'm not breathing. Nope. I'm watching over my shoulder, transfixed as his free hand grabs at the towel still around his waist. Of course, I know what's under there. It's been pressed against me several times, and even now the tent is impossible not to look at. I almost don't register the large tattoo wrapping around his ribs. Some sort of—whatever, it doesn't matter. It's been there all this time and I don't even care about it because he tugs and the fluffy cloth drops, after getting caught for a brief second on his erection.

It's not enormous. That's what I notice, when I'm not squirming my hips around in a pathetic attempt to get him inside me. It's big, of course, because he's big, but it's not out of proportion. If this were a book instead of real life, it would probably be a couple inches longer, a little thicker. None of those details matter. The only thing that does matter is it's his, and it's hard for me.

I make some sort of whimpering sound. Reduced to incoherency and I don't even care. Nothing of the crazy things I've gone through up to this moment matter, because this is the moment I've been trying not to dream about for days.

"Stop moving, Zero, fuck," he grumbles, reaching down to grab my hip and lock me in place.

I can't stop my muscles flexing against him, though. So much pent-up energy is coursing through me, seeking an escape.

"I said stop," he says, accompanied by another spank. It works for all of five seconds, allowing him to kneel on the bed, his knees between my legs to open them up. At least then I have something to struggle against. I throw my legs up as best as I'm able, getting them around his waist and squeezing.

"Hurry," I moan, unable to help myself.

"Fuck, woman, you think I'm not trying? You're like some pixie who drank too much coffee."

How he can be so calm about this is beyond me, and something I file away to bring up later.

He has to take his hand off of my shoulders to grab my hips, leaving me free to get up on my elbows. I swing my head left and right, trying to get the perfect view, but it takes pushing up further and looking underneath, across the length of my body, to see what I want.

His hand fisting his cock at the base, moving hips to get it in the right position. I bite my lip to stop my insane noises as the head of his cock touches my pussy's outer lips. With a little push he parts me, but stops when he's inside enough to be able to let go. My inner muscles are already flexing, trying to pull him in. The soft yet hard tip is maddening, enough to drive me up a wall, but not enough to quench any of the fire boiling inside me.

"Fucking stop teasing me," I yowl like a cat. It's not pretty.

"Calm down, now," he says with infuriating patience. Both his hands are on my hips.

"If you're doing this on purp—"

The rest of what I was going to say is cut off as he slams into me in one thrust, buried to the hilt. I regain my senses to find my tongue hanging out of my mouth, eyes popped open in shock.

"You okay?" he asks. I feel his hot breath on the back of my neck.

"Hng."

"I'll take that as a yes." He thrusts then, full and strong, no soft starts or careful movements to make sure I'm ready. I've never been readier for anything in my entire life, as the extreme wetness in my pussy attests.

As slick as I am, the slide is almost without friction, but it doesn't affect how much he fills me. Stretching to the point of a small burn, which eases down into a tingling warmth with each long stroke. I want to watch, to see his length disappear fully inside me, only to emerge a moment later, but my arms are weak and shaking. I can't control them or myself, flopping face-first into the sheets.

He keeps my hips up, clamped snug in his hands as he continues to drive his cock into me. It shouldn't feel this good, I try to tell myself. You've had sex before. It's just a cock. The lone iceberg of rationality melts in the tropical waters of reality. It's not "just" a cock, it's Lindberg's cock, which makes it worth ten regular cocks.

That bolt of realization overcomes even the feeling of him working in me, if only for a moment. I've never *needed* anyone like this before. Wanted, sure. Been satisfied with, happy around, yes. This feeling of pure animal need is new. He's bypassed all my safeguards and tapped right into the center of my desires.

I need him to throw me around. I need him to spank me. I need him to take control and drive me out of my mind with frustration and carnality.

None of those thoughts are expressed in rational terms. In the moment all I care about is getting fucked by him, hard and strong, until I can't take it anymore.

As if he's reading my mind, I feel his hand slide across my heated skin, and his fingers connect with my clit. They press, then circle. There's no way I can hold back the sounds filling my lungs now, and they tumble out, a waterfall of emotions.

He doesn't say anything, but I can tell. His breath hits my neck faster, hotter, louder. His fingers circle with an urgent need, and his incessant pounding reaches a speed that shouldn't be possible.

I can't do anything but grab the sheets and hold on for dear life. There's no choice in the matter, and no quarter given to my aching pussy. The only thing I can do is climax with him. The slow tremors building up this whole time crescendo into a pulsing supernova that clamps against his hard length. I swear I can feel his heat filling me up, each jet of seed serving to send me to greater heights.

I couldn't say how long it goes on. Minutes, maybe years, but I don't dare stop until with a shout rivaling any of the noises he's made up to this point, he collapses, smashing me to the mattress.

Whatever air was left in my lungs is driven out in a whoosh. If this is how I die, suffocated under Lindberg's heaving and hot body, I guess I wouldn't be unhappy. I don't have to face my end, though, because in a short second he's pushed himself back up. Enough for me to suck in a shaky breath and hold it.

"Good girl, Zero." The words are soft, whispered right in my ear, and this time they don't make my brain heat in anger.

This time they produce a different kind of heat, one I want to feel again and again.

CHAPTER TWENTY-FOUR

Druain

This woman is going to be my undoing. At this moment I'd do anything for her, and that's dangerous. It means I'd be willing to sacrifice everything I've worked for to keep her happy and safe.

The way she's sighing under me, head moving in slow circles as if I've just finished giving her the best neck massage ever, is intoxicating. I'd do anything to see Zero look like this all day, every day. All her crazy stress has washed away, and in its place I'm looking at one satisfied and relaxed woman.

She's facing me, still wriggling under the cage of my arms. I thumb her cheek, stilling her movement so I can kiss her, but even then she still shifts. The touch of skin sliding, muscles moving against my own is almost enough to bring me back to readiness. Her hands wander my back and lower, no pattern to the touch. She still hasn't opened her eyes.

Breaking the silence feels like sacrilege, but if I don't say something soon I'm bound to come up with something really stupid. While I still have control of my mind, and my body is recovering, I need to get control of the situation. If I wait even five more minutes I'll lose myself to her again, and I can't allow myself to succumb to her yet.

"Feeling good?"

Her eyes open like the vault doors to the world's most precious treasure. "Hmm?" Has her voice always been so melodious?

"I asked if you were feeling okay." Slipping a hand behind her back, I shift up into a sitting position, pulling her with me, keeping her close.

Her hands gravitate to my shoulders. For the first time ever she's looking down at me. It's not a position I'm comfortable with, because it's not a position I've ever been in, but being inside her makes it all okay. Her breasts in front of my face also help. If I didn't have this craving in my stomach to keep her as close as possible, I'd be grabbing one.

"I feel okay," she says, toying with the back of my neck, a glint in her eyes. "Do you feel okay?" The last word is accompanied by a squeeze around my semi-erect state.

"You'll have to tell me how I feel," I toss back, attempting a flex of my own. Come on, little buddy, wake back up. I'm ready for round two, three, and however many it takes for her to pass out. I want to fuck her into unconsciousness.

"You feel...okay." The pause right before the "okay" gets my hackles up, but then I notice her chewing on her lip, attempting to hide a smile.

"You're going to pay for that," I whisper in her ear before biting the lobe.

"Promises. You can't seem to do anything now."

I growl and dig my fingers hard into her ass. "Keep at it. I have a good memory."

She squeezes her eyes shut. "What color are my eyes, then?"

"Green. Is this a quiz?"

"What chips did I take?"

"Sour cream and onion." I raise my eyebrows, amused.

"What was the first thing you said to me?"

"That I was going to kill you."

"Do you still want to kill me?"

"Can someone die from too much sex?"

She makes a noise that's a cross between a laugh and an actual purr, then opens her eyes again. "I need to shower."

Caught off guard by the abrupt change of topic when it was headed in a direction I was enjoying, I let her go when she pushes against me. The air is unwelcome and cool against my length as it drops from inside her, coated in slickness.

There's no time to be disappointed, though, since all my focus is on staring at every inch of her body. The way her breasts move as she pushes against the mattress to step off, her long legs unfolding and hitting the floor, her ass as she saunters toward the door. The woman must work out, although I have no idea when she finds the time. She's worthy of statues.

I'll give her ten minutes to wash and then I'm joining her. She looks back at me and I detect a hint of an eyebrow raising. Five minutes.

The moment the door to the bathroom clicks shut I fall back onto the bed and let out a breath. Thoughts of what I'm going to do next spin through my head like a carousel, except instead of horses, a litany of sexual acts, each one dirtier than the last, parade past.

We're doing that one as soon as I can. Definitely that. I hope she's flexible enough for that, because it's happening. She'll survive a little dislocation.

Then unfortunate thoughts of the more distant future surface. What am I going to do about the bodies? How far behind is Costecu? If Gil got here, others are going to get here. Why did he send only Gil, and not come himself at the same time? Maybe I've let my reputation as the best killer slip too much.

I don't panic. I never panic. However, I do stride out into the living room to make sure Costecu isn't already sitting on the couch and waiting for me to show up. He'd have a polite and dangerous smile on his face, and then he'd explain how everything was planned, and then he'd kill Zero over several days and make me watch.

The thought sends me running to check the bathroom and make sure she's still there. I can hear the water, but you never know. Cracking the door open I peek inside. The textured glass of the shower hides all the details, but I can tell it's her. A Zero-shaped figure is hard at work scrubbing.

She bends down to do something, and I almost can't control the urge to crash into the shower and then into her. The panic I'm *not* experiencing is still in control so it makes me close the door with a huge sigh, and I get dressed. All those fun things are going to have to wait, because we're leaving as soon as she's done. We can't delay any longer.

After dressing in the usual button-up and slacks, I check on her again. She's still in the shower, hands up and in her hair. Her profile deserves to be immortalized in some way. Maybe she'd be open to posing for some pictures.

I have to slap myself to turn away. I'll give her five more minutes. Why do women take so long to shower, anyway? I'd have been done ten times by now. I catch myself pacing the front room, nervous energy building in the tips of my fingers and toes. Since I've latched onto the thought of Costecu showing up, I can't let it go. If thinking about it will summon him here then he's about five minutes from showing up.

Wrenching open the front door, I scan the woods. Nothing. Not a sight or smell or sound out of place, which only makes me more nervous, so I make a quick circuit outside, but I don't want to leave Zero alone in the house for too long. The only thing out of place are the dead bodies. Everything else is fine.

Back inside the water is still running. I grumble and move to the kitchen and, needing to do something, I gather food. All the ice cream I bought is going to go to waste, but I'm not it taking it with us. I've piled everything we can take, water on the bottom of the stack, by the front door when the shower stops.

Stuffing back my sigh of relief, I go to open the bathroom door. Zero's standing there, full-on naked, still putting her hair up in a towel.

"Whoa," she shouts, grabbing the other towel and clutching it to her dripping body, scowling at me. "Creep."

It takes everything I have, even with the increasing need to leave, to not take her right there. It would be so easy, and in the mood I'm in, so quick. What's two minutes? I clench my jaw and refuse to give in. Later.

"It's not like I didn't see and touch everything," I say. "There's no need for modesty."

"It's rude. There is such a thing as etiquette." She wraps and tucks the towel around her, making a show of being careful not to let me see anything.

"Not anymore." I could follow it up with my natural thought, which is "You're mine now," but I'm sure it would provoke a fight we can't afford. A fight leading to a fucking that would take more than two minutes. Sighing, I add, "Come on. We need to leave."

"Why?" She puts her hands on her hips.

I grab a wrist and tug her out of the bathroom. "Because I've been an idiot. I was so trapped by your feminine wiles I haven't been smart."

"What—what the fuck does that mean? My *what*?" The rising tone of her voice would be perfect to explore in depth, except the lingering chill in my stomach won't be ignored.

I let another opportunity to banter pass by and pull her into the bedroom to look for clothes. "Costecu's going to be here any minute. I can feel it in my bones. And dwarves have good bones."

She must sense my unease, as she doesn't comment on the softball I've lobbed. "Oh shit. You think so?"

"I know so. I'm surprised he isn't here already. We shouldn't have fucked." The noise of annoyance I'm starting to enjoy, the one I'd fight armies for, floats over my shoulder and I turn to see her scowling.

"Zero, you know I don't mean it that way," I toss at her before digging for a pair of boxers. "We definitely should have, and will many, *many*, more times in the future, but we should've gotten away from here first."

I turn, holding out a green shirt with the black boxers and shove them into her hands. "Put these on. I'm going to load the SUV. Come outside when you're done."

"What the hell? These won't stay on me."

Needing to do something to sate those inner voices, I grab the edge of her towel and yank it off, toss it aside, and then stare at her curves with a critical eye. "Nah, you've got awesome child-bearing hips. There's elastic, they'll stay on. If not, tuck in the shirt. If you're not in the SUV in two minutes, I'll drag you out no matter what state you're dressed in."

She squeak-growls, arms and hands swift to cover her modesty, but I leave the room in a rush. Staying would be dangerous.

Fuck, I want to make love to her so hard. Channeling my energy into loading the SUV, I pick up everything in one scoop, the water, the bag of chips, the cereal, the bread, even the vegetables. I don't plan to be conspicuous and on the road for too long, but if I've got to drive for three days without stopping, we'll at least have something to eat.

Outside the air is still silent, but now it stifles me, invading my lungs like a foul miasma. I'm expecting this rebellion to end at any moment, and each breath is a gift I should enjoy, but knowing Zero is in danger taints what should be peaceful surroundings.

Dumping everything into the back of the SUV without regard to neatness, I run back into the house. I can't wait anymore. It feels like my chest is going to implode from tension, a black hole of dread sucking at my lungs and heart.

Zero is halfway through buttoning up my shirt, looking hot as hell with her miles of legs and lickable curves. Without a word I grab her around the waist and she's back over my shoulder. I could get used to carrying her like this.

"It hasn't been two minutes," she yells, struggling. I'd be disappointed if she didn't.

"Close enough," I retort, dashing back outside, opening the passenger door of the SUV and tossing her in. "We're going now."

"But—"

"The only butt I want to talk about is yours," I shout through the windshield as I jog to my side before hopping in. Closing the door with a satisfying thunk, I start the engine and press the gas. "Because it's an amazing butt."

She opens her mouth to say something, but the speed at which we're traveling does not mix well with the bumpy dirt road. I wouldn't be surprised to see all my teeth rattle out of my skull. The gate is wide open, but I would have crashed through it if it wasn't. We make it to the paved road, and I take the left turn at speed, earning a gasp and a little bump as some part of her hits the door.

Keeping watch on the road in front of us and the road behind, looking for any sign Costecu is on our tail, I miss the question she asks. "What?"

"I said, where are we going? What's the plan?" Her voice is terse, and a glance over reveals the look of determination etched on her features. If I didn't know better, I'd say she's on board with the whole thing. I can't decide if she was being difficult before to egg me on, or if the jolting managed to flip her switch to survival mode. I hope it's the first one.

"I'm not sure yet. Away. Somewhere else."

"You don't have a plan?" Her voice rises on the last word, as if it's the most inconceivable thing she could think of.

"Not really. I tend to think better on my feet. Is that a problem?"

"Oh my god. I'm running away with someone who wings it." She smacks her forehead into the palm of her hand.

"So you are running away with me." The way I say it, it's not a question. It's a statement of fact, one I won't let her refuse. She's going to argue, try to weasel out of it, but I'm not going to let it happen.

"I guess I am," she says after a moment.

All the clever comebacks and refutations I'd planned die in the avalanche roaring through my brain. If Costecu swooped out of the sky and ripped out my heart right now, I'd be okay with it. Zero wants to be with me. I close my mouth before she notices. "Not that you had any choice," I say, attempting to cover my giddy smile with a smirk.

She rolls her eyes. "If I have to be kidnapped by someone, you're not half bad," she mutters, looking away and crossing her arms.

"Was that a compliment? Are you feeling okay? Let me feel your forehead. Do you have a fever?"

She swats away my hand, growling. "Can you not call me 'Zero' anymore? That's not my name, you know."

"I know. You told me after I pulled your toenail off, which I do apologize for." Then I allow myself a small grin. "Although, I did know beforehand."

The look of jaw-dropping surprise and anger on her face is perfect. "You knew the *whole time?*"

I ignore the question and push on with my own path of the conversation. "The problem is, Zero, everyone else calls you Aideen. But I'm not everyone else. If you don't like Zero, you better think of something else."

Her sound of indignation is music to my ears as we drive north, fleeing danger together.

SNEAK PEEK
Aideen and Drew's adventure continues in *Darkness Exposed*
Turn the page...

DARKNESS EXPOSED

We're fleeing to who knows where with no plan and no idea if anyone is chasing us. The forest flashes by on either side of the one-lane highway as I stare out my window. I should be afraid, or at least worried, but all that's reflected back at me is determination and a tinge of excitement. This is the most impulsive and dangerous thing I've ever done, and the high hasn't worn off yet. The high of sex and violence. I keep expecting myself to come to my senses, snap out of it, demand to be taken home so I can sort everything out.

The minutes tick by and I say nothing.

"What are you thinking, Zero?" Lindberg's low rumble breaks into my musing.

"Miss Duffy" might be a bit formal, but is it too much to ask he at least call me Aideen? He seems determined to stick with the nickname he came up with after he kidnapped me from the secret prison where I'd locked him up. It's hard enough to believe it's only been a couple hours since our adult activities, but it's even more unbelievable it's only been a few days since this whole thing started.

What a simple time it was. I was content with my job of protecting humans from rogue creatures like Lindberg and his boss. With the help of the organization I'm a part of—we'll get to whether I'm still part of them—we investigate and lock up all sorts of criminals from werewolves to vampires to ghouls. I used to be able to take regular baths, something I'm missing more and more with every hour. Showers are fine, but for a selkie like me, nothing quite beats submerging in a tub full of water and letting all my tension and injuries disappear down the drain.

Any wounds I have can be cured by water, be it a bath, a shower, the ocean, or rain. I haven't tested things like limb removal, but broken bones have been painfully reknit together. Even as recently as yesterday I was repaired when Lindberg's shower fixed the fingers on my hand he'd snapped when interrogating me in front of Costecu.

Yet here I am, being driven by the man who broke my fingers and pulled out my toenail, all because he ignites this flame in my stomach and other more intimate parts. He was pretty good at the whole sex thing. Even made sure I was taken care of first.

"Zero?" he asks again.

"What? Oh. Nothing."

"I don't believe that," he says, reaching out and grabbing a lock of my hair, trailing his fingers down as it drapes over my shoulder, and then giving a tug.

"Ow, you jerk." I grab at the sting in my head and turn to scowl to cover my secret and worrying desire to have him pull it harder. I never wanted to get a tattoo because I was scared of the pain, yet around Lindberg everything is flipped. I shove down the forceful memory of those three hard spanks he'd applied to my ass. "What are you, five?"

"You know you like it." His grin is infuriating.

"Shut up. No, I don't."

His reply is cut off by a curse as a deer gallops across the road in front of us, sunlight dappling across its hide. My heart leaps in surprise as the SUV swerves to avoid hitting the animal, and I almost bang my head on the window from the sudden movement.

Lindberg stops on the shoulder. "You okay?"

"Yeah," I say. "Startled."

"Sorry. My driving skills aren't what they used to be."

"Driving skills? You mean besides pushing the pedals and moving the steering wheel?"

He ignores my question, staring at me with the intense gaze I'm learning means he's thinking about something. "You know I'm the one who's been feeding you information from the inside, right?"

"Yep. I figured that out. Somewhere around the second corpse."

He grunts in a non-committal way and pulls back onto the road. "Did you ever meet my handler?"

Glancing at him out of the corner of my eye, trying to decide where this line of questioning is going, I shrug. "No. Whoever it is reports to higher-ups, and they filter the information down. For security reasons. Why?"

"Curious." His fingers beat an arrhythmic staccato on the fake leather steering wheel. "You know, she—"

Whatever he was going to say next is interrupted by a massive crash, shattering glass, crunching metal, a jumble of sharp and discordant sounds. It's so sudden I don't notice for several suspended seconds that we're tumbling through the air, rolling over and over, flinging me in every direction possible.

As sudden as the crash starts it ends, with a final creak and groan of metal. Through my window is sky, through Lindberg's window is pavement. My seatbelt holds me in place, dangling to the side, cutting into my hip and neck. The airbags are flaccid, having given their lives to keep us from bashing our brains out against the dashboard.

There's too many wrong things to notice at once: steam from the wrecked engine in front of us. Pain in my knee, head, and arm. Lindberg with a grimace on his face, a cut across his forehead, his hands still gripping the wheel.

"Fuck. Get out, Zero," he croaks.

"You're bleeding."

"Get out. Now."

Something in his tone brooks no argument. It's a tone he's used only a couple times before, and always for a reason. I grab at my buckle, click it open, and tumble to land on him.

"Sorry," I say, trying to get my feet under me on the center console without stepping on him so I can open my door.

"Oof."

Flinging the door open only for it to crash to the ground, I pull myself up, wiggling across the battered metal of the passenger side of the SUV and drop to the ground. Standing leaves me a little dizzy, as if seeing the SUV on its side is somehow tilting my world. I rub my forehead to try to clear the lingering confusion of the accident, ignoring the aches. There's water in the vehicle. I can use that to heal whatever minor injuries I might have.

I notice the other car at the same time Lindberg starts yelling again. Of course, there had to be another car, what else would we have hit? Before I can run over and make sure the people are okay, shouts pierce the fog still enveloping my brain.

"Zero. Get away. Get away." His voice becomes clearer on the last shout as his head emerges from the passenger-side opening.

It's enough to take a split-second to assess the situation, taking in everything like I'm trained to do. The accident shook me up, but some semblance of observational skill limps back.

The SUV we were in is on its side, but I can see the huge dent in the rear driver's side quadrant from where I'm standing. It's right where it should be to spin a car out. The other vehicle is a black SUV similar to ours, and the damage on the front of it has been absorbed by the massive grill, which is now hanging off and dented.

There are no skid marks on the pavement where the crash happened.

Movement in the other SUV catches my eye. Four people shaking off the impact. No panicked looks, no open mouths of shock or apology. Large people.

"Zero," Lindberg shouts again.

ABOUT THE AUTHOR

Cyprus Hart's earliest memory of trying to become a writer involves carrying a clipboard around and asking family members if the name "Rock Stone" was a good name for an action hero. Fast-forward three decades and he's still convinced he can make it work.

When he's not writing kissing, and other activities along those lines, into every book, he's tries to keep his border collie entertained and keep him and his chihuahua warm in the frozen tundra of Missouri.

Sorry – he doesn't like coffee *or* tea.

Connect with Cyprus:
website: www.cyprushart.com
IG: @AuthorCyprusHart
twitter: @CyprusHart

www.BOROUGHSPUBLISHINGGROUP.com

If you enjoyed this book, please write a review. Our authors appreciate the feedback, and it helps future readers find books they love. We welcome your comments and invite you to send them to info@boroughspublishinggroup.com. Follow us on Facebook, Twitter and Instagram, and be sure to sign up for our newsletter for surprises and new releases from your favorite authors.

Are you an aspiring writer? Check out www.boroughspublishinggroup.com/submit and see if we can help you make your dreams come true.